Happy New Year!

I hope 2007 is going to be a great New Year for you. It certainly is going to be an exciting year for Harlequin Romance! We'll be bringing you:

More of what you love!

From February, six Harlequin Romances will be hitting the shelves every month. You'll find stories from your favorite authors, as well as some exciting new names, too!

A new date for your diary…

From February, you will find your Harlequin Romance books on sale from the **middle of the month.** (Instead of the beginning of the month.)

Most important, Harlequin Romance will continue to offer the kinds of stories you love—and more! From royalty to ranchers, bumps to babies, big cities to exotic desert kingdoms, these are emotional and uplifting stories, from the heart, for the heart!

So make a date with Harlequin Romance— in the middle of each month—and we promise it will be the most romantic date you'll make!

Happy reading!

Kimberley Young
Senior Editor

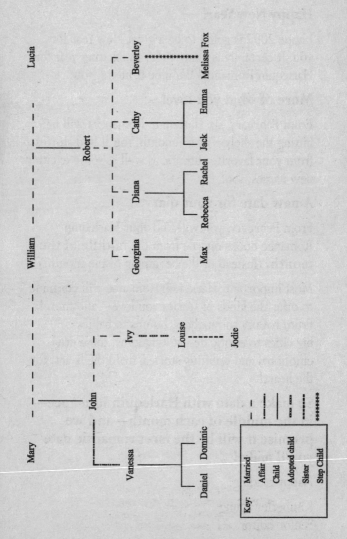

Key:
Married	————
Affair	—·—·—
Child	————
Adopted child	———
Sister	·········
Step Child	********

BARBARA MCMAHON

The Nanny and the Sheikh

The Brides of Bella Lucia

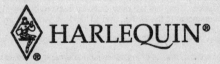

HARLEQUIN®

TORONTO • NEW YORK • LONDON
AMSTERDAM • PARIS • SYDNEY • HAMBURG
STOCKHOLM • ATHENS • TOKYO • MILAN • MADRID
PRAGUE • WARSAW • BUDAPEST • AUCKLAND

ISBN-13: 978-0-373-03928-9
ISBN-10:   0-373-03928-X

THE NANNY AND THE SHEIKH

First North American Publication 2007.

Copyright © 2006 by Harlequin Books S.A.

Special thanks and acknowledgment are given
to Barbara McMahon for her contribution
to *The Brides of Bella Lucia* series.

This edition published by arrangement with Harlequin Books S.A.

® and TM are trademarks of the publisher. Trademarks indicated with
® are registered in the United States Patent and Trademark Office, the
Canadian Trade Marks Office and in other countries.

www.eHarlequin.com

Printed in U.S.A.

THE BRIDES OF BELLA LUCIA

A family torn apart by secrets, reunited by marriage

First there was double the excitement as we met twins Rebecca and Rachel Valentine

Having the Frenchman's Baby—Rebecca Winters
Coming Home to the Cowboy—
Patricia Thayer

Then we joined Emma Valentine as she got a royal welcome in September

The Rebel Prince—Raye Morgan

There was a trip to the Outback to meet Louise Valentine's long-lost sister, Jodie

Wanted: Outback Wife—Ally Blake

On cold November nights, we caught up with newcomer Daniel Valentine

Married Under the Mistletoe—Linda Goodnight

Christmas was the time to snuggle up with sexy Jack Valentine

Crazy About the Boss—Teresa Southwick

Now, join Melissa as she starts the New Year by heading off to a desert kingdom

The Nanny and the Sheikh—Barbara McMahon

And don't miss the thrilling end to the Valentine saga in February

The Valentine Bride—Liz Fielding

To Pat McLaughlin—a long-distance friend dear to my heart! Thank goodness for phones!

CHAPTER ONE

MELISSA FOX threw down her pencil and rubbed her eyes. Arching her back, she tried to relieve the tense muscles. Translating business documents wasn't the most stimulating activity. She shook her head and took a deep breath, glancing around the crowded office of Bella Lucia. The headquarters for the famous London restaurant group was a busy place. The accountants had their own row, quieter than where she was working. The general manager had a private office. She was seated in an extra desk near the receptionist who fielded a gazillion phone calls a day.

But she shouldn't complain. She was between jobs and thankful to have something to do. Her mother had obtained this assignment for her through her new husband. It was only temporary, until mid-February when she flew to the United States to take on a new family.

A professional nanny, Melissa had recently quit her job as childcare resident at a large international hotel in Lake Geneva. She'd been there for five years, and had loved every minute. Or, almost every moment. Until the debacle with Paul. Now she planned to move on to working as nanny to a single family. The McDonalds were expecting their third child in February. When they had met her last fall in Switzerland, they'd talked her into accepting an assignment with them when the new baby arrived.

After the end of her relationship with Paul, she was ready to change. Their current nanny was planning to marry in late January and the timing would be perfect.

Melissa looked back at the lengthy document. She was almost finished. She would complete the translation today before heading home. At loose ends since quitting her job just before the holidays, she was grateful for the chance to earn some money until she took up her new position. But she missed the children and the activities and her friends in Switzerland. Still, the chance to spend some time with her mother was great.

Staring at the page, she let her mind wander a bit. When her mother had prevailed upon her new husband, Robert Valentine, to offer Melissa a temporary job, Robert's oldest son, Max, had come up with a spot in the office for the exclusive Bella Lucia restaurant business. She'd started by filing, then answering the phones. Once Max had discovered she was fluent in French, he had immediately started her on translating a stack of documents he had received from Sheikh Surim Al-Thani who lived in Qu'Arim, an Arabic country on the Persian Gulf. Apparently the two men had been corresponding for some time about the feasibility of opening a Bella Lucia restaurant in Qu'Arim. Sheikh Surim Al-Thani and Max wrote their letters in English. It was the construction firm giving preliminary bids who used French.

Working with the translations, Melissa was learning a great deal about the restaurant business and how Max envisioned the operations to run. She cross-referenced the documents with the correspondence between Max and the sheikh. It was a new venture for the family-owned and -operated restaurants—expanding in a foreign market. She knew Max had mentioned opening a few more worldwide if this one proved successful. Maybe he'd open one in Boston one day—near enough that she could visit while she was employed by the McDonald family.

She picked up her pencil to begin again. Only a few more paragraphs.

The sheikh was building a luxury resort right on the Gulf. The restaurant would be the jewel in the crown of the new holiday destination, he'd said. He had plans to make the entire seaside complex the premier place to visit in that part of the world.

Melissa wished wistfully that she could visit herself. It was rainy and cold in London. Switzerland, where she'd lived the last few years, was buried in snow. How wonderful would it be to visit a tropical resort in January, laze around on the beach, visit souks and find exotic goods at rock-bottom prices?

The McDonald family lived in Massachusetts, which was also under snow. Apparently she was destined to live in cold climes.

Max came up to her desk.

"Got a moment?" he asked.

"Sure, what's up?" She still wasn't used to the fact that Max Valentine was her new stepbrother, but already liked him very much. He was tall, dark and handsome, and, though her own feelings toward him were purely platonic, she could see why Max had more than one woman in the office preening every time he walked through.

"Come back into my office if you would."

Melissa followed him into his office and sat on one of the visitor chairs.

He leaned back in his own chair studying her for a moment, a small smile playing around his mouth. "I have to fly to Qu'Arim on Sunday as I'm meeting Surim for a final session before we sign all the paperwork. They've already started building and I'd like to see the setup. It's thanks to the translations you've done that we've got a lot of the preliminary work behind us, so…" he paused "…how would you like to come with me?"

"To Qu'Arim? I'd love to!" Melissa felt a surge of excitement. Look out beaches, she was on her way! How terrific of Max to offer her the chance. It would be more like a vacation than work. And a fabulous opportunity to see more of the world.

"It will only be for a week and I expect to return home by

the following weekend. We'll stay with Surim.' Max smiled. "His home is large enough for a battalion."

"You've been there?"

"Several times. He stays with me when he's in London. He and I went to Eton together. Until our final year."

"What happened then?" Melissa asked, intrigued to learn she might get to meet a real-live sheikh and that he had actually gone to school in her country.

"His father died and he had to return home and assume the role of leader before we graduated."

"At sixteen or seventeen? How could anyone that young rule a country?"

"He was young, but had lots of advisors," said Max. "By diligently working with the various factions in his country over the years, he's been able to pull the country into a united front. Which probably saved its economy at the same time."

"Isn't Qu'Arim known for oil and pearls?" she asked. She'd read up on the country when she'd first begun the translations.

Max nodded. "And fishing. Their pearl industry used to contribute a bigger percentage to their wealth, but money from oil far outweighs it now. Consequently that industry gets bigger press. But high-quality pearls from Qu'Arim are well known and sought after by experts." He stood up, signaling the end of the conversation. "Anyway, plan on staying a week. And you'll need to bring something dressy—if I know Surim, we'll attend at least one reception. We'll leave early Sunday."

Melissa nodded and rose, almost dancing with delight. "I appreciate this, Max."

"You'll be helping me out. If that contractor has anything new to report, I'll need to have an instant translator. You're up to speed on where we stand, so you'll be more valuable than anyone new to the project who could translate," Max said, grinning at her obvious excitement.

Melissa smiled back and left, and as she tidied her desk her bright smile refused to fade. She was going to Qu'Arim! She loved to travel and see new sights. She'd visited much of Europe on holidays, but she'd never been to the Middle East with its exotic and mysterious settings. And what better time of year to escape the rain and cold of London?

It was dark by the time she left the building a short time later. She stared at the dreary January weather, wondering if she could catch a cab or was destined to take the underground and then walk the few blocks to the house. She had her umbrella, but the thought of splashing through cold puddles for several blocks held no appeal. Instead, she dwelt on the thought that in only a few days she'd be in sunshine and warmth.

When Melissa reached home, she was disappointed to find it empty. She was anxious to share her good news. Her mother and Robert had probably gone to an afternoon matinee or something. Robert and her mum were in the honeymoon stage, having been married less than a year. While she was glad for her mum—it had been far too long since her own father had died—nevertheless sometimes she felt left out.

Had things gone differently with Paul, Melissa might have been the one in the early stages of marital bliss. She'd been so wrong in her judgement. It made her wary now of trusting her instincts. She refused to think about the man any longer. He was in her past, and she was a wiser woman because of it.

Shaking off gloomy thoughts, she went upstairs to her room. She had time to shower and change before dinner. She wondered if she could find further information about Qu'Arim on the Internet. It was one thing to read casually about the country for work, something else to learn all she could before actually visiting the place.

Sunday morning, Max and Melissa caught an early flight to Rome where they changed for a plane to Qu'Arim. It was late afternoon when they landed. Immediately after exiting the plane, Melissa raised her face to the sun. Its warmth felt fabulous! The air was perfumed with the sweet scent of plumeria mixed with that of airplane fuel. The soft breeze that wafted across her skin felt as silky as down. Soon they'd be away from the airport and she could really enjoy scents that vied for identification.

"I already love it here," she said as they walked across the tarmac.

"Did you say something?" Max asked, a bit distracted. He was in full business mode, having worked on the plane and now carrying his briefcase almost as if it were a part of him. Melissa wasn't surprised. The man loved his work. He ate, slept and breathed it as far as she could tell. Though, he wasn't a hermit. He did his fair share of dating, according to her mother.

"It's nice here," she said, trying to match his businesslike attitude. Inside, however, she felt sheer excitement. She hoped she had some free time to explore while she was here. And maybe spend an afternoon at the beach. The Persian Gulf had been a heavenly blue when they had circled preparing to land.

They were met inside the terminal by a tall man with dark hair and almost black eyes. He smiled at Max when he spotted him and Melissa felt her heart skip a beat. She'd thought Max handsome, but this guy was something else! His charcoal-gray suit and red power tie were very western. She glanced around; most of the men wore suits, few wore the more traditional Arab robes.

In fact, she could have been in any airport in Europe. For a moment she was disappointed. She wanted to see more of the exotic aspects of this country, not find it was just like any other capital she'd seen.

Melissa spotted two men standing nearby, scanning the crowd. The local equivalent of guards, she guessed from the way they behaved.

Max turned and made the introductions. Sheikh Surim Al-Thani inclined his head slightly, reaching for Melissa's hand

and bringing it to his lips. The warmth of his lips startled her, but it was the compelling gaze in those dark eyes that mesmerized. She felt her heart race, heat flooded through her and she wondered if he came with a warning label—dangerous to a woman's equilibrium.

"Welcome to Qu'Arim," he said formally, his voice deep and smooth with the faintest hint of accent. "I hope your stay will be enjoyable. Please let me know if there is anything I can provide for you while you are here."

"Thank you," Melissa mumbled, feeling halfway infatuated by the sheer animal magnetism she sensed in the man. She could listen to him all day. His hand was warm and firm, almost seeming to caress before he released hers. She felt a fluttering of awareness at his intensity when he looked at her. Giving herself a mental shake, she tried to think of the mundane reason for her visit. She was definitely not here to get a crush on Max's friend.

She glanced back and forth between the two men as they spoke. Both carried an air of assurance and confidence that was as appealing as their looks. But it was Surim who captured her attention. Before she could think about it further, their host gestured toward the entrance.

Their small group began to move toward the front of the airport. She gladly let Max and Surim talk together while she looked eagerly around, taking in the crowds of travelers in the various dress. There was a mixture of languages, some she recognized as European. She wondered how hard it would be to learn some Arabic while she was here.

Melissa and Max were ushered into a luxurious stretch limousine while one of the men attending the sheikh went to fetch their luggage. Melissa settled back in her seat and gazed at the landscape, trying to ignore the growing sense of awareness she felt around the sheikh. He joined them after speaking to his men and Melissa was hard-pressed not to stare. Resolutely she gazed out the window.

Flowers and soaring palms lined the avenue, softening the austere lines of the airport terminal.

As the sheikh continued his discussion with Max as the limo pulled away from the airport she occasionally glanced in his direction, intrigued as never before. Surim Al-Thani was slightly shorter than Max, but at six feet still towered over her own five feet three inches. His dark hair gleamed. She wondered if it was as thick and silky as it looked.

When he met her gaze she felt flustered. She had been rude. Yet when his eyes caught hers for an instant she continued boldly staring—this time directly into his dark gaze. Growing uncomfortably warm, Melissa finally broke contact and again looked out the side window. Her heart skipped a beat, then pounded gently in her chest. Concentrate on the scenery, she told herself, meaning that outside view, not the handsome sheikh who sat opposite her.

She wished she'd questioned Max more about their host. While working with the children in the resort in Switzerland, she'd met all levels of society. This attraction wasn't due to his wealth, or even his power. He was simply one sexy man and Melissa wondered how much she'd get to see him during their visit. The less the better, she was starting to think.

The thoroughfares were wide and straight, with banks of flowers in the center islands. Because the limousine's windows were closed to contain the air-conditioning, she couldn't tell if the flowers she saw were the ones that smelled so fragrant at the airport. But their bright blossoms danced on the breeze.

She wasn't listening to the conversation, but became aware of when it stopped. Glancing away from the window, she saw both men looking at her.

"Did I miss something?" she asked.

"I was telling Surim that your fluency in French is why I brought you," Max said.

"It is the second language here in Qu'Arim, though English is gaining favor," Surim said in French.

She wondered if he was testing her. She replied in the same language, "It was the primary language where I worked before, so I have become quite proficient. I'm the one who translated the documents from the construction firm that you sent to Max recently."

He inclined his head in acknowledgment. Returning to English, he glanced at Max. "I hope you will be pleased with the site I've chosen for Bella Lucia. It is right on the water, with palm trees framing the view. We can drive by before heading home if you like."

Max quickly agreed.

Melissa felt she wouldn't mind seeing the site herself. Right on the water—it sounded fabulous.

And it was. The construction site was quiet. The framing of the main building had begun, concrete had been poured, pipes were sticking up in various locations. Max and Surim donned hard hats and headed for the far end of the building.

"You stay out of the construction site," Surim said to Melissa.

Another time she might have been annoyed at such a high-handed command, but she was too enchanted with the setting to care. She would much rather walk down to the water's edge than traipse through a construction zone any day.

The driver of the limo leaned against the hood and watched the men. The two men who had been with the sheikh at the airport had followed them in a separate vehicle. One remained with that car, the other hurried to catch up with Surim and Max. Apparently they took their security seriously, though there was not another soul in sight.

Melissa climbed out of the limo and headed for the water. Her shoes were not at all suitable for the sand, so she kicked them off. Her stockings would undoubtedly be sandy when she put the shoes back on, but she'd deal with that later.

The sugar-white sand was soft and warm. She found the going easier when she reached the damp hard-packed sand near the water's edge. The deep blue of the Persian Gulf stretched before her. She drank in the clean air, relishing the slight salty tang. Turning, she studied the outline of the resort. The main building would be three stories tall, with a high roof. She could see the men at the far end where the restaurant must be situated. Palm trees fluttered in the breeze. It was an ideal setting.

Looking left and right, she was amazed there weren't scores of families enjoying the beach. But as far as she could see in either direction, it was pristine and empty.

She'd love to go swimming, but that was totally out of the question. At least for today. Would she get time off while they were here? She needed to remember she'd come to work, not vacation. But the water was so tempting.

Glancing around, she saw Max and Surim heading for the car. Reluctantly, she returned as well, dusting off her feet as best she could before donning her shoes.

"Enjoying yourself?" Surim asked when they reached the limousine.

She met his glance as she slipped her feet into her shoes. Did she detect a hint of amusement? "It's fantastic. But I'm puzzled why the beach is so empty. I'd think hordes of people would enjoy a day here."

"That is my hope as well, once the resort is completed. In the meantime, construction holds certain danger, so I have closed the area for the duration of building," Surim said.

"I see." All that lovely empty beach. She sighed. There went her idea for swimming.

They resumed their places in the limo and in only a short time they turned into a long driveway flanked on either side by tall palms. Melissa looked with interest at Surim's estate. She had no idea of what kind of place a sheikh might own. Somehow she'd thought maybe a lavish tent like in *Arabian Nights*.

The edifice surprised her. Max hadn't been exaggerating when he'd said it was large enough for a battalion—it was huge. Whitewashed walls with terra-cotta trim reflected the bright sunshine. High arches of windows, outlined by ornate fretwork and mosaics inlaid in bright colours, provided symmetry on the front. A wide veranda seemed to encircle the entire three-story structure. Quite simply, it was stunning.

"It's beautiful," she said, now taking in the colorful flowers that grew in profusion right to the edge of the veranda. Gently waving palm trees encircled the house, while a lush lawn stretched out in all directions. Her gaze was drawn to an elegant fountain in the front, providing a focal point to the circular drive. The watery spray made dozens of sparkling rainbows. She sighed wistfully. What a magnificent place to live.

"Are you near the Gulf?" she asked, not seeing any signs of the sea, but still smelling that slightly salty tang in the air even in the car.

"There is a path from the back of the house that leads to a private beach. It is not far, only a short walk," Surim said. "Perhaps you'd care to go for a swim sometime during your visit."

She smiled at him. "Yes, I would. It's freezing in London right now." Would he join her if she went swimming? She looked away, afraid he'd see the hope in her eyes.

As she followed her host into the house a moment later, through large acacia wood double doors carved into intricate designs and polished to a gleaming shine, she wondered why Max had brought her since Surim spoke French fluently. To have an impartial person on his side? Not that she could imagine the sheikh being the slightest bit dishonorable. Of course he was probably too busy to translate mere construction documents.

Or, as her mother had suggested, maybe the trip was a treat for the work she had already done. It didn't matter; she was thrilled to be here.

The interior of the house was cool, though not apparently due to artificial means. Windows were wide open allowing a balmy breeze to flow through. The tall ceilings allowed the air to circulate freely.

Rich colorful furnishings filled the room to the left. She followed the men and stood in the doorway, her sandy stockings starting to annoy her. How soon could she escape to her room and change?

"You must be tired from the journey," Surim said. "I'll have my housekeeper show you to your room. Dinner will be at eight."

"Thank you," Melissa said, glancing at Max to make sure her departure would be all right with him. There wouldn't be any work today, would there? Surely if he and the sheikh were such old friends they had lots to catch up on.

"Good idea. That'll give you and me time to look over the plans. I've noted some changes I want in the kitchen area," Max said.

So much for catching up on their personal lives. Was work the only thing these men cared about?

Melissa pulled back the cool sheets from the high bed. It was after eleven and she was tired. Slipping beneath the light covers, she lay back on the mattress, her head still swimming from the conversation at dinner. It had only been the three of them in the ornate dining room that could have seated fifty-four easily. The primary topic of conversation had been the new restaurant and resort.

She would have preferred an alfresco meal on the veranda, with more talk about Qu'Arim to enable her to learn more about the country. Maybe with another guest or two to round out the numbers. It was apparent the sheikh liked things formal. It was a good thing she was only here a week; the protocol would drive her crazy.

After dinner, she'd excused herself to wander in the gardens. They'd been illuminated with subdued lighting. She'd walked down one path and then another, exploring little nooks and thoroughly enjoying herself. It was such a change from wintery London.

Melissa began settling on the pillow, her eyes closing as she reviewed what she needed to remember for the morning. They would eat at seven and head for Surim's offices where she and Max would meet with the contractor. Then they would—

A sudden shriek startled her. She sat up. What had that been?

Listening intently, she heard another shriek and then a child crying.

The sheikh wasn't married, at least not that she knew. But that was definitely a child. She got up and found her robe, pulling it on as she hurried to her door.

Opening it, she could clearly hear the wailing. It came from the third floor.

Her heart hurt to hear a child cry so wretchedly. She ran lightly down the hall to the stairs she had seen earlier and quickly gained the third floor. Rushing to an open doorway, the light spilling into the hall, Melissa halted at the scene before her.

Surim had shed his jacket and rolled up the sleeves of his dress shirt. His hands were on his hips and he glared at three young children huddled on a sofa. An older woman stood near a door on the opposite wall, wringing her hands. The oldest child looked to be seven or eight, a toddler leaned against her. It was the little boy, about four or five, who was crying so hard.

Without a thought, Melissa stormed into the room.

"What is going on?" she asked. Moving past Surim, she gathered the little boy in her arms, brushing back his hair and hugging him as she sat on the edge of the bed. "What's the matter, little man?" she asked in her most soothing tone.

The other two children looked at her with startled surprise, then glanced nervously at Surim.

Melissa turned, the little boy in her arms, and glared at the sheikh.

"These children should have been in bed long ago; it's after eleven," she said in her firmest nanny tone.

"That is what I have been telling them," Surim said, his own voice showing his frustration. "Their nurse has been unable to control them. When Hamid awoke with a nightmare, he woke the others. Now they won't return to bed. If they don't behave, I'll have to find new accommodations for them."

"That's the coldest thing I ever heard a father say!" she exclaimed.

"I'm not their father," he returned.

The little boy rested his head on Melissa's shoulder, quieting. She hugged him again and looked at the other two. They looked tired, scared and wary.

"Well, whose children are they and why were they left with you?" Melissa asked. The woman moaned slightly and lowered her gaze.

Surim lowered his hands and took a step closer, anger evident in his eyes.

"My household is not your concern. You are merely a guest. Here because Max requested it."

"Children are my concern, however, and if you can't take proper care of these children, I shall report you," she replied hotly. The foolishness of the comment struck her. Surim was the leader of the entire country. To whom would she report him?

Surim narrowed his eyes, anger threatening to choke him. Then the absurdity of what she'd just said penetrated. His anger immediately cooled. For a moment he thought he'd challenge her on that. He looked at Melissa, then at the children. They shrank away from him. He was not a monster. He would never strike a child. Yet they walked as if on eggshells around him.

No wonder—he had no clue how to care for children. He'd hired Annis to watch them. But they were proving too much for her. Not that he had any intention of sharing that information with his guest. Maybe boarding schools were the answer.

He looked back at Melissa. She might be petite, but she

looked as if she'd fight him to the death. And she didn't even know the children.

"These are my cousin's children. Nadia, Hamid, and Alaya. They have come to live with me recently and we haven't found our way yet. I would prefer you not report me." Surim let the humor of the situation defuse the tension. He had never heard anyone in Qu'Arim threaten to report him before. The novelty was priceless.

"Perhaps they should return home," Melissa said.

"Unfortunately, their parents were killed in a car crash and they have no home to return to. As their guardian, I now provide for them."

Surim watched as Melissa shifted Hamid in her arms. He had to be growing heavy. At least she had been able to stop his crying, for which Surim was grateful. The nightmares came regularly and Annis seemed incapable of doing anything to stop them. Not that he himself had been any help. Yet Max's little friend seemed to have the knack of quieting the child. He'd take any help he could get at this point.

He looked at her once more, surprised to see she was in a gown and robe. Her hair looked soft and touchable, her eyes sparkled with righteousness indignation. And the color that rose in her cheeks intrigued him.

Max had asked if his assistant could come, more for a holiday than for needed work. Was there something between the two of them? Surim had not seen anything. Which didn't mean she was totally unattached. Was there a man waiting for her in London?

"Perhaps you'd help get the children settled for the night," he said, dragging his speculation back to the matter at hand. With a glance at Annis, he shook his head. The nurse had proved most ineffective when dealing with these children. How hard could it be to put three children to bed at a reasonable time each night? Weren't nurses supposed to be able to deal with nightmares and other problems Hamid seemed to have?

"Perhaps I should." Melissa looked at the two girls. "Hi, I'm Melissa. Want to help me get Hamid to bed? Then I'll tuck you both in and read you all a story."

"Our room is across the hall," the older girl said. "Hamid couldn't hear the story from his room."

"Then tonight why don't we have all three of you sleep together, and then everyone can hear at once?"

"I wuv stories," the littlest one said.

"They speak English," Melissa said, looking at Surim.

"Their parents lived in England. They were all three born there," he replied.

"Ah, I'm from England, too," she told the children. "Let me tell you about the weather when I left, cold and rainy. They even thought there might be snow in the north before the end of the week. It's much nicer here."

Surim watched as the Englishwoman seemed to effortlessly gather the children to her and head them to the girls' room. In a moment all he heard was her soft murmur.

"I'm sorry they disturbed you, Your Excellency. The boy had a nightmare and the girls awoke to come to his aid," Annis said in Arabic.

Surim sighed. This was the fifth or sixth time since they'd arrived it had happened. When would it stop?

"It is to be expected, I suppose. We will discuss the situation in the morning," he said.

The older woman scurried away. Surim wished she'd shown a little of the backbone Melissa Fox had when she'd taken him to task. Annis had come highly recommended, but Surim didn't think much of her abilities with these children. Unlike Melissa Fox, who had miraculously charmed them all.

Himself included?

Report him, indeed.

He crossed the hall and paused near the opened door. The three children were snuggled together in the large bed. Melissa sat in a chair near the head, reading a story. Already little Nadia had her eyes closed. Hamid was fighting sleep.

Surim watched as Melissa seemed to calm them all, and bring much-needed rest.

He waited until she checked the children, gently closed the book, and turned off the light. She made it seem easy. Yet he had no idea of what to talk about to a child.

When she stepped into the hallway, she was surprised to see him.

"Thank you for getting them to sleep," he said formally. He was embarrassed a guest in his home had had to involve herself with his responsibilities. But the quiet was much appreciated. He hoped they slept through the night this time.

"I apologize for speaking to you as I did earlier. It was not my place," she said, equally formally, looking just beyond his left ear.

It was a perfect apology, but he didn't believe she really meant it. From the stiff way she held herself, he had an idea she'd like to tear into him and berate him for not being a better guardian for the children.

"I hope they will not interrupt your visit a second time," he said politely.

She flashed him an annoyed look and turned to walk down the hall. "Children don't annoy me."

Lucky her, that children didn't annoy her. Or baffle her as they did him. He expected them to do as they were told, but had found in the three weeks they'd been in his home that expectation was not met more times than it was.

He glanced into the darkened room once more, feeling a sharp pang at the thought of his cousin Mara's death. She and her husband had been too young. And he had never expected to be named guardian of three children under the age of nine. He knew nothing about children. He'd have his secretary begin researching boarding schools in the morning. There had to be some that would take children as young as two.

CHAPTER TWO

MELISSA dressed in a navy suit and sensible shoes the next morning. She and Max were meeting with the contractor at Surim's offices. Then they would all view the site again, with the foreman explaining each stage. She would begin to earn her salary today. That was if Surim would still let her work. Melissa sighed. She really shouldn't have threatened him last night. Would he mention the incident to Max? She needed to watch her tongue and not blurt out things before thinking.

Breakfast was served buffet-style in the dining room. Max was sitting in the spot he'd occupied last night when Melissa entered. After a quick glance around, she breathed a sigh of relief. Surim was not present.

"Good morning. I hope I'm not late," she said to Max.

"Not at all." He looked up from the English newspaper he was reading, hot tea steaming by his hand. "Surim left a while ago. He'll meet us when we get to the office. Help yourself to breakfast."

Melissa didn't know if Surim normally ate a hearty English breakfast or had had one set out for his guests, but she gladly dove in. The amount of food out on the sideboard for two people was staggering, yet she saw no sign of the children. She wondered if they'd slept through the night without further incident.

"What do you think of Qu'Arim so far?" Max asked when she sat opposite him. He folded his paper and laid it aside.

Melissa smiled. "About what I expected with a country that has such strong ties with Europe. The downtown buildings are taller than I expected and much more modern. Overall it looks very prosperous. And I especially love the flowers that grow in such profusion."

"Surim's done a terrific job. He was telling me about his plans for expanding their tourist market, which is the reason for the resort. He has an aggressive schedule devised to lure in European and American money. If anyone can pull it off, he can."

"That's why he wants Bella Lucia?"

"Of course. Anyone from the UK will recognize the name. As we stand for the highest quality it will be a strong draw he wants for the initial guests," Max said.

She nodded, glancing at the doorway as she strained to hear any sounds from the children. But the house remained silent. Were they still sleeping? She'd like to spend more time with them. She hadn't realized how much she'd miss children until she'd taken this extended break between her old job and her new. It was the longest she'd gone without interacting with small children since she'd finished her training.

"I'm ready when you are," Max said, folding his napkin.

Melissa took a final swallow of her coffee and stood. "Let's go."

They had the limo at their disposal and as they were driven through the city streets Melissa felt a hint of excitement at the thought of seeing Surim again. He hadn't paid her much attention yesterday, and she'd been rude last night. Still, there was a fascination that hadn't been quelled yet. She'd love to talk to him about his country, about how he felt taking the reins of leadership so young. What changes had he made? What were the plans for the future?

It wasn't his looks alone that fascinated her. He was a

challenge to talk to, seemed smarter than most men she had dated, and carried himself with confidence bordering on arrogance. Yet on him it sat well. She tried to pinpoint exactly why she felt drawn to the man. He definitely didn't have a way with children. But many men left most of the childraising to the wife. He had lots more going for him than being father of the year.

"Max, did you know Surim has three children living with him?" she asked.

"Umm? Children? I don't think so; he's not married. Though I heard he's looking."

"Maybe because he has those three children," Melissa said. What did that mean, looking? Could she ask without giving the impression it was important?

"What children?" he said, looking at her.

"Their parents just died. They were raised in the UK and speak English as well as you or I do."

Max looked at her in puzzlement. "How do you know this?"

"Didn't you hear them last night? The little boy woke from a nightmare and was crying loud enough I heard him in my room."

"I didn't hear anything." He looked pensive. "I can't imagine Surim with children. Running a country, yes. Visiting Europe and squiring beautiful women around, yes. Kids, I don't think so."

"No surprise there. He didn't seem to have an ounce of sympathy for the little boy." She tried to maintain her indignation, but couldn't help thinking of Surim's side of things. If he wasn't used to being around children, becoming an instant guardian to three would be daunting.

The limo stopped in front of a large high-rise glass and steel skyscraper. Max led the way and Melissa hurried to keep up. Tall people never seemed to consider that those not blessed with extraordinary height would have trouble keeping pace.

Entering a mirrored elevator, they were soon whisked to the top floor. Stepping out onto a luxurious carpet, Melissa gazed around, noting the old paintings on the walls, the elegance of the furnishings and the quiet hum of business.

She and Max were ushered into a conference room. The outer wall was of glass, offering a spectacular view of the Gulf. Melissa wanted to stand there and drink in the sight, but Surim was already at the large table with three other men. Introductions were quickly made—the contractor and his assistant, and Surim's project manager. All the men from Qu'Arim spoke French, so they used that language, Melissa translating into English for Max.

When she wasn't speaking, she studied Surim. He had the capacity to totally focus on the situation at hand. Did he bring that focus to his new children?

Would he bring that focus to a woman? She could imagine being the center of his attention; his eyes would gaze into hers. His conversation would be on topics she liked. And the woman would feel like a queen. Not that she would ever know. Not that she wanted to even venture there. She'd been burned badly by Paul and had no intention of flirting with a friend of Max's. Max had trusted her enough to bring her as his assistant; she would do nothing to damage that relationship. How awkward it would be if Surim complained Melissa was flirting with him. She cringed at the thought.

But she couldn't help glancing his way again. And came up against his gaze focused on her. He didn't read minds, did he?

When it was time to go to the construction site, Melissa rode with Surim in his private car, which he drove. Max went with the others in the limo.

"I wished to speak to you privately," Surim said as they merged into traffic.

"About?" For a moment, despite her best efforts of keeping a businesslike demeanor, her imagination soared. Would he reach out and take her hand? Tell her he was delighted she'd joined Max and would she spend time with him alone before they returned to England? Maybe she'd like to see a quiet place only he knew?

"To thank you for calming young Hamid last night. He has been troubled by nightmares a great deal."

Her bubble popped.

"Not unexpected if he just lost his parents," she said, feeling foolish after all. Thankfully no one else knew of her dumb daydreams. She really had to get control of her emotions. Paul should have cured her once and for all of getting ideas about rich, powerful men and their interest in a nanny. Especially with the cultural differences added in.

Surim nodded, focused on driving.

"Perhaps. I hope they won't bother you tonight," he said.

"No bother. I'm sorry they are going through such a trying time. It was fortunate they have family to take them in."

"My cousin's mother, Tante Tazil, is not well. She is unable to care for them. But I don't believe they will remain with me for long. I have my secretary looking into boarding schools."

"What? They're too young to be sent away!" Good thing she didn't have any illusions about the man; this would have shattered any lingering ones. Who would think of sending babies to boarding school?

"I went to boarding school when I was nine, in England—which was a foreign country to me. We are looking at schools in England. That is their native country, even though their parents were from Qu'Arim. They have been raised there and I thought it would make them feel better to be back there."

"Nadia is still a baby, Hamid can't be five yet and Alaya is still too young to be sent away. Think, Surim, they are *children*. They have just suffered a horrific loss of both parents. Being here took them away from the only home they knew, and now you're proposing to shunt them off to some school—if you can even find one that will take them that young."

"I'm sure that will not be a problem."

The arrogant statement caused Melissa's blood to boil. Men who were obscenely rich thought money could buy everything. But not family ties, not love and loyalty, nor negation of his responsibility to his cousin's children.

"Maybe not to you, but think of them," she said. "It would be horrible."

"They are unhappy and disruptive. During the day they run wild around the house, yelling and breaking things. At night Hamid has nightmares and awakens the entire household. Their nurse cannot control them. I believe a more structured environment would be beneficial. It is not open for discussion; I was merely informing you of my plans."

They had reached the site of the hotel and he turned to park beside the row of cars and trucks near the building. The activity at the site was a stark contrast to yesterday. The lot was crowded with workers. Trucks of cement were dumping their loads. Men and machines worked as if choreographed, building a structure that would reflect the desires of their sheikh to expand tourism for his country.

Melissa ignored it all, however. She was so angry she could spit! How dared he mess those children around like that? They needed stability and love, guidance and assurance that they were part of a family—not to be sent away from the only relative who was apparently able to look after them.

She reached out and caught his arm, stopping him from exiting the car.

He looked at her with some surprise.

Amazed at her own audacity, she nonetheless held onto her courage. "There has to be other alternatives. Think, please. They're babies. They need comforting, love. You are their cousin, their guardian. Spend time with them or find other family members who can care for them. Don't send them to some institutional school so far away."

"I believe I know what is best for the children." He slipped his arm from beneath her hand and climbed out of the car.

"I don't think so," she muttered, opening her own door and getting out before he could come around to assist. Her opinion of the man dropped significantly! How could he do that to those precious children?

Max had said he was looking for a wife. Maybe his attitude was one of the reasons he wasn't already married.

Yet her heart ached for those sweet children. Maybe she'd find a way to make him change his mind.

Melissa was tired by the time she and Max returned to Surim's house in the late afternoon. Dinner would not be for a couple of hours. She quickly showered and put on some casual, light trousers. No one had said she couldn't visit the children, so she went up to the third floor.

They were sitting in front of a television, the program in Arabic. Why weren't they outside in the sunshine?

"Hi," she said, stepping inside the room.

All three kids scrambled to their feet and rushed to greet her.

"You came back," Alaya said in perfect English. "I didn't think we'd see you again. I'm sorry Hamid woke everyone up last night."

"I had a nightmare," the little boy said.

Nadia held up her arms and Melissa scooped her up, hugging her gently, then resting her on her hip.

"What are you doing inside on such a gorgeous day? I heard there's a path to the beach," Melissa said. She smiled at the older woman sitting with crochet work in hand.

"Do you mind if I take the children out for a walk?" she asked in French.

With the nurse's agreement, she told the children to get

ready. "We'll walk there and back. But only on the condition you are on your best behavior," she admonished, remembering what Surim had said about their running wild.

"We haven't been outside except to the gardens. Annis doesn't like to go far. She's old," Alaya ended in a whisper.

"Well, I'm not and I'm up for a walk to the beach. Sun cream first and then we'll leave," Melissa said. The nurse wasn't that old—she looked to be about fifty—but to a young girl she probably did seem elderly.

The outing proved to be full of fun. Melissa forgot about being tired and held Nadia's and Hamid's hands. Alaya walked on the other side of Nadia, chatting freely.

"We've been here a long time it seems and never seen the beach. Our parents died, you know. I really miss Mummy. Is the water cold?" Alaya asked.

"I think it's warm. We'll find out together." Melissa found the gate leading out of the garden and followed the neatly kept path. In only five minutes they reached a pristine stretch of beach totally empty in both directions. The children ran toward the water.

"Don't go in until I get there," Melissa called, running after them. It felt so good to be free of office clothes, to be running in the sunshine. The laughter of the children warmed her heart. She was glad she'd followed her instincts and sought them out.

The children kicked off their shoes and waded in the warm sea. Melissa quickly followed, getting the bottoms of her trouser legs wet, but she didn't care. She was happy to enjoy the excitement of the children.

"I want to go swimming," Hamid said, splashing his sisters.

"Whoa, not so much water. Another day we'll ask about swimming. How about we race along the water's edge? Who can run the fastest?" Melissa said, looking to channel some of their energy. They probably got into trouble in the house from sheer curiosity and exuberance. She'd make sure they got enough exercise to sleep soundly tonight.

"Me," little Nadia said.

"I can," Hamid said.

They were off, running at the edge of the water, splashing and laughing. Alaya took off after them, with Melissa following.

When they tired of that, Melissa suggested they build a sandcastle.

Alaya looked sad. "Mummy and Daddy built a fabulous one the last holiday we had. We went to Cornwall."

"I'm sure they'll be happy to see you are building a new sandcastle on this beach. It's a long way from Cornwall, but sand is sand. Won't you join us?" Melissa wasn't exactly sure what to say to grieving children, but she knew it was good for the children to talk about their parents.

"You can tell us how to make one like your mummy and daddy built. Did you help them?" she asked.

Alaya nodded. "I miss them." She started to cry. The other two ran to her, upset by their older sister's tears.

Melissa reached out to draw her into her arms, hugging her warmly. "I know you do. You will miss them all your life. My daddy died when I was five and I still miss him. But the aching, crushing hurt will diminish, I promise. One day you'll look back at all your memories so grateful to have them. They'll bring smiles to your face and a lift of love to your heart." Melissa wished she had more memories of her father. Alaya was older than she'd been. She would remember. But the others would not. It was so sad.

"I miss Mummy, too," Hamid said.

Melissa sat on the sand, pulling Alaya down with her, and keeping one arm around her shoulder. She patted her lap and Nadia climbed on, while Hamid crowded from the other side. She wished she could hold each one until the hurt eased.

"Of course you miss them. They were your parents and loved you very much. You know they didn't want to die."

"It was a truck, crashing into them," Alaya said. "The

brakes failed, that's what the policeman said. Why did it have to happen?"

"No one knows things like that, sweetheart," Melissa murmured. "But you will be cared for here."

"Nobody here knew our parents or talks about them. It's as if they were never alive," Alaya said.

"Your uncle knew your mother. Get him to talk about her and your father. I bet he has wonderful stories about when they were young," Melissa suggested.

"He's our cousin," Alaya said, bitterness tingeing her voice. "He doesn't want us. Mummy asked him long ago to be our guardian if something happened to them and he said yes. But he doesn't want us."

"He's your family," Melissa said, hoping it wasn't a total lie. "He's just not used to children. We need to find a way to have him feel more comfortable around you."

"He's getting married," Hamid said, looking up at her. "Will she be our new mummy?"

"No, we are not getting another mother," Alaya said firmly.

Nadia slipped her thumb into her mouth, watching with large eyes.

"Because of the age difference, I'm sure the sheikh wouldn't mind if you called him Uncle Surim. His new wife will be your new aunt. Have you met her yet?"

"He's looking," Alaya said.

"Looking?"

"He needs to get married to have sons to carry on when he dies," Alaya said.

"But he's not going to die soon," Hamid said, looking at his sister. "Is he?"

"No, he has to get married first," Alaya said.

"How do you know this?" Melissa asked, curious.

Alaya and Hamid looked away.

"Sometimes we spy on him," she said in a low voice.

"We sneak down the stairs and listen at the door, then run like the wind when someone leaves the office room," Hamid said.

Melissa was torn between laughter at the picture, and telling them that spying wasn't really a good thing.

"So he wants babies. They'll be new cousins for you to play with," she said, wondering why he was planning to send these adorable children away if he wanted children of his own. She hoped he found his wife soon, and she'd insist on keeping the children.

Paul's scathing denouncement echoed in her mind. He hadn't wanted children at all. He considered her involvement with them immature and beneath a woman he'd want to marry. For a moment she was back in the small restaurant hearing his voice, feeling each word as a dart piercing her heart. She'd thought they had so much going for them, until she'd voiced that thought and been soundly corrected. How had she misjudged him so much?

Shaking off the melancholy, she smiled.

"Let's get going on those sandcastles. Dinner will be soon and we'll have to return to the house."

The children scrambled up and ran to the water's edge again. Soon they were all mounding wet sand, trying to sculpt it with fingers. Melissa made a mental note to see if there were sand toys in the children's nursery for future visits to the seashore.

Surim walked down the path to the beach alone. Annis had come to tell him the children had not returned in time for their supper. She was worried she'd done the wrong thing by allowing them to go off with his guest. Sometimes it was almost more than he could do to control his frustration. His aunt had insisted Annis be hired to watch her grandchildren. But however qualified Annis appeared on paper, her skill with the children lacked a great deal in his opinion.

As he approached the beach he heard laughter and happy chatter. Pausing by the last of the green grass, he observed four people caught up in building a sandcastle. Little Nadia for once didn't have her thumb in her mouth. Hamid was laughing so hard he fell over and rolled on the sand. Alaya stood, running to the water to scoop some in her hands and carry it, dripping all the way, back to the ditch they'd built around the castle.

But the person he had the most difficulty recognizing was Melissa Fox. She looked like one of the children. Gone was her suit and her business attitude. Her hair was flying in the breeze, and her trousers were damp and sandy. He could see the joy in her expression. He was struck by how beautiful she was. Suddenly he was gripped with an urge to see her dressed in a designer gown, with pearls from Qu'Arim at her throat.

Every one of them was having so much fun a pang of envy struck. Surim couldn't remember the last time he'd laughed like that. Or spent a carefree afternoon doing nothing more important than building a sandcastle.

Hamid rolled to his knees and caught sight of Surim. The merriment dropped instantly from his face. He said something and the others looked his way. Alaya stopped smiling and stepped closer to Melissa. Nadia popped her thumb back into her mouth and regarded him warily.

Was he frightening to these children? He remembered his cousin Mara fondly. They'd played together when he was younger—not any older than Hamid. He'd seen her often when home from school, before his father had died and his life had changed so drastically. He'd never expected her to die young, or for himself to wind up responsible for her children.

Melissa rose, dusting some of the sand from her clothes.

"Are we late?" she called. She spoke to the children and as one they turned to walk to the water and swish their hands clean. Picking up their shoes, they moved to stand just behind her. In a moment, the little line headed his way, almost like a mother duck with her ducklings following in a row.

Surim watched, fascinated at the change in his guest and the laughter he'd seen from the children. He had only seen them sad or scared or defiant. Melissa still looked carefree and happy, but the children had become solemn.

"Annis was worried when they didn't return for dinner," he said when Melissa drew close.

"Sorry about that. I forgot my watch. Guess my estimating the time from the sun isn't very accurate." She laughed. "But we were having such fun time seemed to fly."

He looked at the pile of sand, then at the children. "A very fine castle," he said awkwardly.

"I bet you and their mother made sandcastles when you were young," Melissa said.

He was startled. He hadn't said anything about Mara or her husband, fearing to upset the children.

"Did you?" Alaya asked hesitantly.

Surim regarded the little girl and nodded. "We did. And when we grew older, we had swimming races, and went water-skiing together. She and I were great friends during the summers when I was home," he said, remembering back before the world had changed and his childhood had ended abruptly.

"Where were you in not summer?" Hamid asked.

"I went to school in England. Where you used to live."

"I miss home," Hamid said forlornly.

"This will feel like home in no time," Melissa said bracingly. "Right?" She smiled brightly at Surim.

He raised an eyebrow at her comment.

She smelled like sunshine and salt air. He noticed the deep green of her eyes, the glossy shine to her hair. There was a faint hint of pink on her cheeks—from the sun? She was shorter than most of the woman he dated, and much too young. But for a moment awareness flared.

Intellect didn't rule the body all the time. He remembered how soft her skin had felt when he'd kissed her hand at the airport, a gesture foreign to him. Had he been making a show for Max's friend?

Instinctively it had seemed right.

The children marched quietly into the house, all evidence of the joy he'd seen subdued by his presence. Surim wished he could change that.

"I'll run up with the children and give Annis a hand getting them cleaned up," Melissa said when they reached the stairs.

"Our own dinner will be in thirty minutes."

"Then I'll have to hurry." She herded the children up the stairs without another glance in his direction.

For an instant, Surim wished she'd been as eager for his company as she was for the children's. He had no trouble in the romance department. Though none of the women he knew held the same appeal that Melissa held.

He was being pressured by several factions to take a wife, and have children to insure the dynasty. These days he seemed to be looking at every woman with the same question—could he live with her for the next fifty or so years? So far he hadn't found anyone.

Melissa slipped into the dining-room chair just as Surim and Max came in from the study. Once they were seated, a servant entered from the kitchen with a platter of meat. Melissa had rushed through her ablutions; her hair was still damp. But she had not kept the sheikh waiting for his meal.

She listened as Surim and Max discussed business, wondering what other activities the sheikh participated in. He had to take women out if he was looking for a wife. Did he discuss business with them? Or was it all romance?

She wondered what a date with him would be like, what they would talk about. Did he discuss the orphan children in his care with them? Or maybe he concentrated on wooing the woman, delaying any talk of family until he decided she was the one.

In the meantime, perhaps she should offer some suggestions to getting to know the children? She shook her head, hiding a wry smile. As if he'd listen to her. Who was she to advise the ruler of Qu'Arim? He had advisors galore. And a perfectly qualified nurse in residence. Though what the children needed was love and devotion and fun. And a chance to get to know Surim and establish new family routines and traditions.

"You're quiet tonight," Surim said, addressing her. "Too much activity today?"

Melissa looked up. "Oh, no. I enjoyed seeing the actual site of the new restaurant, and the plans you have for the resort. I'm sure it will be spectacular."

"Of course it will," Max said. "Surim doesn't do things by half measures."

"I thought to have a small gathering of friends and advisors before you leave. Most of them speak English, the ones who don't speak French," Surim said.

"I would like the opportunity to meet your friends here," Max said. "I already know most of your friends in England."

"And you, Melissa, would that please you?" Surim asked.

"I should be delighted to attend." She wondered if he would bring one of his potential wives with him, and she was disturbed to realize how much the thought bothered her.

When dinner finished, they moved to the drawing room. As they walked Surim and Max continued their discussion of the possibility of expanding Bella Lucia beyond this one overseas restaurant.

Passing through the wide entry hall, Melissa heard a noise. Neither of the men seemed to notice. Glancing up, she spotted Hamid peering between the railings of the balustrade. She looked at Surim and Max. They were too engrossed in their conversation to hear such a slight noise.

When they reached the living room, Melissa paused at the doorway.

"If you two will excuse me, I think I'll go on up."

Surim looked at her, frowning. "I apologize that our conversation centered on business. You must be tired of it after the long day we put in. We will change the topic."

"No, you two talk all you want. Max won't be here that long and I know you're friends from way back. I'll see you in the morning."

His dark eyes seemed to hold her gaze as he weighed her words. "Very well." With a slight inclination of his head, he turned back to Max.

Hurrying up the stairs, Melissa caught Hamid and Alaya as they tried to run down the hall.

"Hey, you two, stop right there." She kept her voice low, but knew the children heard her.

They stopped and looked back, nervously waiting as Melissa went to them.

"I thought we talked earlier about not spying," Melissa said in her sternest voice.

"We wanted to see you tonight," Alaya said.

"Do you know where my room is?"

Alaya nodded.

"In the future, wait there if you need to see me. Or leave me a note. But no more spying; it's wrong."

Alaya nodded. Hamid looked at his sister, then nodded solemnly as well.

"Now, what's up?" Melissa asked, smiling at the children.

"We wanted to see if you would read us a story," Hamid said. "Annis only reads in French and we don't understand."

"Or she speaks Arabic and we only know a few words that Mummy and Daddy taught us," Alaya said.

"You will need to learn the language if you're staying here," Melissa said. She started walking to the stairs leading to the third floor. "Maybe we'll ask Annis to start Arabic lessons in the morning. Tonight, I'm happy to read you a story. Is Nadia already in bed?"

"Yes. She was sleeping when we came down," Alaya said. "I wish we didn't have to stay here. Everything's so different from home."

"You'll get used to things in time, then it will be like having two homes. The one you had in England, and your new one here. Do you have friends back at home?" Melissa asked.

Alaya nodded.

"Have you written to them about your new place?"

The little girl shook her head.

"That would be fun for them to receive a letter from you telling them all about this house, your uncle and Annis. I bet none of them have ever been to Qu'Arim. Maybe you could get some photos to include in the letter." Melissa smiled as the enthusiasm started to show on Alaya's face. "This house is fantastic. Just a photo of the front would look like a museum or something."

"I'd like to write to Sally and Marta. You think they'd write back to me?" she asked wistfully.

"I'm sure of it. First thing tomorrow, I'll have Annis make sure you have paper and pencil. You write as much as you wish and then we'll get your uncle to post it," Melissa said.

"I should be delighted," Surim said behind them.

CHAPTER THREE

MELISSA turned around, surprised. "I thought you and Max were in the living room."

"He had a call to make before it got too late in London. I thought I heard voices, so came to investigate." He looked at Alaya. "If you wish me to post a letter, I'm happy to do so."

"Thank you, Uncle Surim," she said shyly, moving closer to Melissa.

"Uncle? We're cousins," he explained.

"Easier for them if you're Uncle Surim and your new bride will be their new aunt." Speaking softly, Melissa leaned closer. "They don't want a replacement for their parents just yet."

He raised an eyebrow. "My new bride," he said evenly.

Melissa swallowed. Was that some secret? She shouldn't have said that.

"I heard you were looking for a wife," she said, feeling embarrassed, as if she'd been caught gossiping behind his back.

His face was impassive. "That is the plan."

Heat turning her face bright red, Melissa was thankful when Hamid interrupted. "Melissa is going to read us a story," he said firmly. "Come on, Melissa."

"You have a way with the children," Surim said. "Don't let them pester you."

She glanced sharply at him. "They aren't pestering me, for

heaven's sake. They just want some adult attention. You should be reading them their stories. Annis's English is limited. She only reads French stories; they don't understand those."

"She speaks English," he said, his brow creasing.

"And stop frowning, it scares them," she said.

He looked at her in astonishment.

Melissa almost cringed. She needed to watch her tongue or she'd be asked to leave so fast her head would swim. This was a sheikh, not some bumbling idiot.

"Sorry, but I do think you should try smiling more." She bit her lip and looked at Alaya.

Surim stooped down until he was at a level with Hamid. "Should I read to you?" he asked gently.

Melissa was the astonished one. She'd never heard such gentleness in Surim's voice, nor expected him to do something so kind to a little boy.

Hamid seemed undecided. "Can you both read to us?"

Surim smiled and nodded, glancing up at Melissa.

Melissa was struck dumb. When he smiled his entire face changed. He looked younger. And much more appealing. A flutter of nerves centered in her stomach. He would have no trouble wooing some woman to become his wife if he smiled at her once a day.

Rising to his full height, he continued looking at Melissa, a hint of amusement in those dark eyes. "You have a way with children; do you have any of your own?"

"Of course not, I'm not married."

"Neither am I, but I seem to have acquired three."

Melissa wanted to point out he planned to ship them off to some school, but she kept quiet, conscious of the presence of the two children. Maybe if Surim spent some more time with them, he'd find he couldn't send them away.

"Come on, then, let's read these children to sleep," he said.

It was oddly intimate, Melissa thought, to be with Surim

tucking the children in bed. Almost as if they were the children's parents. Surim had dismissed Annis when she'd rushed out to see to the children. Melissa glanced across the bed to watch as he patted Hamid on his small shoulders. She thought it was the first time for the man.

"Sleep through the night, little one," Surim said, almost as an order.

Melissa hid a smile. He might be trying, but his manner needed polishing.

She selected two books, and handed one to Surim. "Want to start?" she asked.

"Ladies first. Besides, if they fall asleep on your watch, I don't have to read."

She laughed. "Very well."

His strategy worked. Before Melissa finished the book she'd selected, both children were fast asleep.

"Tomorrow night, you can read the first book," Melissa whispered as they left the bedroom.

"I would never be able to put as much enthusiasm into reading. Nor come up with different voices for the different characters. You have a talent for working with children."

"I should, it's my job."

"What do you mean?"

"I'm a nanny by profession."

He paused at the top of the stairs. "I thought you were a translator."

"Max very kindly found me some work between jobs—at my mother's insistence, I'm sure. She recently married Max's father, you know."

Surim nodded.

"Anyway, I finished my last job before Christmas and my next one doesn't start until February, so I'm helping out at Bella Lucia. They obviously knew I had no experience in anything except childcare, so Max found this job for me. I speak French and Italian and a smattering of German. I needed it when I lived in Switzerland."

"Where is your next job?"

"In Boston, Massachusetts, in the United States."

"I'm familiar with Boston," he said dryly. "Quite a change from Switzerland."

"And from what I've been doing. Until now, I worked at a childcare facility at one of the resorts in Switzerland. You know, come for a week and let us take care of your children so you can enjoy all the amenities. It was great fun, but now I want to try working for a family. When the McDonalds asked me, I jumped at the chance. It's what I was trained for." She had no intention of letting anyone know part of the reason for her desire for change was a love affair gone bad. So far she'd kept that secret.

"Perhaps you can offer me some insights into these children before you leave," Surim said, continuing down the stairs.

Melissa walked beside him, wondering how much she had to offer in the few days remaining. Still, if she could get them all comfortable around each other, that would go a long way.

"Perhaps," she said at last.

When they reached the door to her bedroom, he paused. She reached to open it. Surim stopped her, turning her to face him.

"Thank you for your help. The children seemed happier tonight than they have since they arrived."

To her surprise, he kissed her. His lips touched hers lightly, then he stood back. "Don't tell Max I'm taking advantage of his new stepsister. He'd have my head."

He turned and walked down the hall.

Melissa blinked, still not sure of what had happened. Her lips still felt the brief warmth of Surim's. Her head was spinning. And the way her heart pounded, she couldn't have imagined it.

Yet how astonishing.

In a haze, she entered her bedroom.

* * *

Surim continued down the hall, wondering what had come over him. He had dated some beautiful, sophisticated women. Enjoyed their company, their sparkling repartee. But he'd never kissed them on such short provocation. Melissa was kissable. He'd wanted to kiss her since he saw her laughing on the beach that afternoon.

She was nothing like the women he usually dated. His advisors and ministers would have a fit if they knew of his interest. Not that a kiss to thank her for her help with the children would endanger the country.

Was that all it was? A thank-you kiss? He was not a man to give embraces so freely.

Yet when he'd seen Melissa going up the stairs with his wards, he'd wanted to join them. Alaya and Hamid seemed quiet and awkward around him, but they blossomed around Melissa. He almost felt he could blossom around her. Shed the duties of office and enjoy an hour or two with her without the constant pressure of duty.

Unlike Annis, she seemed to have a real rapport with children. They'd all looked so happy at the beach. Then Alaya and Hamid sought her out after dinner. To his knowledge none of the children had ever sought him out.

He remembered how small Hamid had felt when he'd tucked him in. His shoulders were so frail in Surim's stronger hands. What would the boy do when he grew up? Would he want to travel as his parents did, or be content to find work in Qu'Arim and make a life here?

For a moment the thought of influencing all three children in how they grew and what they became was daunting. Yet he knew he had to marry soon and beget heirs for his own family, and for a future ruler of Qu'Arim. How effective he proved as a father would influence the lives of his own children.

And where would he find a woman to become the mother of those children? He had been enjoying the company of women for years, yet had never found a special woman to invite to share his life. He had given up on the elusive love that westerners believed in. A suitable union with a woman from a fine family would produce the heirs he needed. As long as they were compatible.

He knew women sought him out because of his wealth and power. Somehow he couldn't see Melissa being impressed by either. In fact, she didn't seem impressed by him at all. No one in recent memory had scolded him as she had.

He almost smiled when he remembered her fussing at him. She was a champion of those children. For a moment he wondered what it would be like to have her champion him.

He returned to the salon and his friend Max. Another complication—if Max found out Surim was kissing his newly acquired stepsister. Better to keep his distance. Melissa was only visiting for a week. Then she'd return to London and he'd resume his quest for a wife.

On Tuesday, Melissa and Max were the only two at breakfast again.

"Surim keeps early hours," she murmured as she took some eggs and bacon. She liked saying his name. Far from being daunted by the sheikh, after that brief kiss last night, Melissa was becoming more fascinated. He'd insisted that first day that she call him by name. Now she looked for ways to use it.

Max sipped his hot coffee and looked up from the paper he was reading. "He's putting in long hours because we're here. I saw him before he left; he said the small reception he's planning will be Thursday night. We'll fly home on Friday."

"Everything going all right?" she asked, sitting at the table.

Max nodded, his face serious. "Surim has done all the preliminary work as we discussed. Today I want to spend time with the contractor, reviewing the specs, and trying to convey to him the ambience I'm looking for, what a Bella Lucia Restaurant means beyond the fixtures."

Melissa's services were dispensed with around two o'clock. She was driven back to Surim's home where she went up to change and go find the children.

Annis was happy to have her take them for a walk. Once the three children were ready, they trooped down the stairs, chattering happily. Alaya confided she'd written her friends, Hamid talked about swimming and Nadia babbled quietly to herself, smiling up at Melissa from time to time.

They walked through the garden and to the beach. The afternoon was perfect and Melissa wished Surim had taken some time to spend with the children in such a carefree manner. If he could just get to know them, she knew he'd fall in love with them. She was halfway in love with them herself.

But Surim didn't join them for the afternoon, nor for dinner. Learning the men would return late, Melissa elected to eat with Annis and the children. After they were in bed, she went for a walk by herself in the gardens.

The paths were illuminated and she enjoyed the quiet of the evening, the air warm even after sunset. She sat on one of the benches for a long time, soaking in the atmosphere, enjoying the fragrant flowers. She found it so amazing to be enjoying this garden in January. How wonderful to have such a residence. It seemed to her Surim wasn't home enough to enjoy it.

Wednesday was a repeat of the previous day. Melissa regretted not seeing Surim, but she needed to keep this visit in perspective. She was not here to be entertained, but to help Max where she could. And when he didn't need her services, she loved spending time with the children.

Still, she wished Surim would make a few moments in the day to see the children. She'd half a mind to speak to him about it. Or was that just an excuse to see him again?

Thursday was the last day they'd work at the site. Max had booked their flight for early Friday morning. Melissa walked through the resort one last time, wondering if she'd get to come back some day when it was completed and see the final result. She knew from the drawings and plans it would be spectacular. Perhaps one day she'd return and take a tour.

The reception Surim had promised was to be held in the large ballroom on the left side of the main entryway of his house. Melissa had brought a suitable dress, but requested time to look for another that afternoon to take advantage of some of the boutiques she'd seen on the main thoroughfare. The limo had been put at her disposal. She stopped on the way back from the new hotel site at a boutique she'd seen each day and found the perfect new gown for the evening. It was floor-length dark blue silk and fit as if it had been made for her. Her black heels would have to do, as she didn't have time to find a shoe store.

After a quick snack in her room, Melissa dressed for the evening. She hoped she looked suitable enough to be entertained by a sheikh. A bit nervous, she was about to go downstairs when there was a knock on her door.

Alaya, Hamid and Nadia stood in the hall grinning at her.

"Oh, you look beautiful. Mummy used to get dressed up to go to parties," Alaya said sadly. "Annis said we could come to see you before we went to bed. I wish you were reading our story tonight."

"Oh, honey, I do, too. But your uncle has put on this party and I don't want to disappoint him, either. Besides, you can read to the other two. That would be good practice for your reading, and give your brother and sister happy memories."

"I guess. Will we see you tomorrow before you go?"

"I'll come up to say goodbye," Melissa promised, already feeling sad to have to bid farewell to these special children. "You'll have to write to me to make sure I keep up with what you are doing. And get your uncle to take photos so I can see how fast you grow."

"I don't want you to go," Hamid said.

"I know. But I'll write to you from England, and then from America. Won't that be fun?"

He shrugged, not looking at all convinced.

"Is anything wrong?" Surim asked, coming down the hall.

The children jumped and moved closer together.

"Not at all, they just came to see me before the party," Melissa said.

She looked up and almost stared. She loved the way Surim looked in his tuxedo; his broad shoulders filled out the suit to perfection. The white ruffled shirt made him seem all the more masculine and exciting. His tanned skin was a startling contrast to the pristine white.

His dark eyes sought hers and held her gaze for a long moment. Her heart fluttered and she became suddenly self-conscious. She'd thought she'd become used to gorgeous men when seeing Valentine family members. None could hold a candle to Surim.

"You look nice, too, Uncle Surim," Alaya said shyly.

Melissa narrowed her eyes sharply, hoping that overture would be returned in the manner meant.

"Thank you, Alaya. It's always nice to have a compliment from a lovely young woman," he said gravely.

Melissa wanted to applaud.

"Nicely said. Now, children, scoot up to bed. I'll see you in the morning," she said.

They each gave her a hug and then walked wide around their uncle and broke into a run for the stairs.

"You intimidate them," Melissa said, falling into step with him as they walked downstairs. The first guests would be arriving momentarily.

"I know little about children," he said.

"Spend time with them. Laugh with them and show them you care. You're their closest relative, right?"

"Their grandmother also lives in Qu'Arim. She is in frail health, however, so cannot care for them."

"Do they see her often?"

"No. They haven't seen her since the funeral."

He stopped at the top of the stairs. Lifting her hand, he kissed the back softly. "You look beautiful tonight."

"Thank you. And thank you for having the reception. I look forward to meeting others from your country."

"I've neglected you during your visit. You should have seen more of Qu'Arim."

"We were here for business," she said, wondering if he realized he still held her hand. "Perhaps I'll come another time and be able to see more."

"Perhaps." He let her hand go and escorted her down the stairs.

Melissa tried to quell the riotous sensations that flooded through her at his touch. It was a good thing they were leaving in the morning. She was infatuated with the man; staying any longer would put her heart at serious risk!

They reached the foyer just as the first guests arrived. Melissa excused herself from the sheikh and went into the reception room. She smiled when she thought about the children coming to see her dressed up. In the few days she'd known them, she'd grown so fond of them. Her heart ached at their loss, and the fact their guardian seemed so remote. They needed to be hugged, laughed with, and convinced they were cherished.

Melissa could relate because of her own father's death. She remembered how she'd felt when she'd finally realized she would never see her father again. All these years, and she still felt the loss. She couldn't imagine losing her mother as well.

The opulent drawing room began to fill. Melissa stood on the sidelines, watching the elegantly dressed women and splendidly attired men enter, talking, laughing softly. It was a wonderful gathering. She wondered whom among them Surim counted as close friends. Did he do what her friends did—go clubbing, or skiing? Was he a water buff, living so close to the Gulf? Or did he prefer more challenging activities like mountain climbing? Did he ever go into the desert and watch the stars from places far from man-made lights? She wished she knew more about her enigmatic host. For a moment she was lost in a daydream of Surim taking her to a quiet, secluded spot to share his thoughts and dreams with her.

"Madam?" A stately gentleman stood next to her.

"Yes?" Melissa smiled. He appeared to be in his late seventies, but still had a luxurious head of thick gray hair. His skin looked like burnished teak.

"His Excellency said you are from England. I am to make myself available to you for anything you may require," he said with a slight bow. "I am Asid ibn Tarvor at your service. I spent many years in England. I am especially fond of your Lake District."

"As am I," Melissa said with a smile. "How nice to meet you."

"Have you been long in Qu'Arim?"

"No, only a few days, and I've been working with the sheikh, though I have managed a few afternoons at the beach. What I've seen of the country is amazing."

Asid took her around, introducing her to others. After a brief exchange each time, they'd move on to the next group until Melissa felt she'd met everyone there.

They stopped near a small alcove.

"Have you visited one of our pearl farms?" Asid asked.

Melissa shook her head. Just then she caught a glimpse of Surim escorting a lovely woman whose dark hair was elaborately coiffed and who wore a beautiful golden gown that enhanced her voluptuous figure.

Asid noticed her glance and smiled. "Ah, Delleah. She is lovely, do you not think? It is time Surim took a wife."

Melissa nodded politely at the comment. Was this the woman he would marry? Or was he still looking?

She hoped the latter; she'd hate to think he was promised

to someone and kissed her! But, if Delleah was the woman
Surim chose, she would make a beautiful wife. They were a
stunning couple.

"I see Asid found you," Surim said as he and the woman at
his side stopped in front of Melissa.

"Indeed, it was most kind of you to think about me. I
would have been fine on my own, but Asid and I have had a
most delightful discussion." She smiled politely at the woman
at his side.

"May I present Delleah bin Attulla. Delleah, a friend from
England, Melissa Fox. She is proving invaluable in the work
we are doing at the new resort."

"Hardly that," Melissa said, greeting the woman.

Delleah's flashing dark eyes and pout did not bode well for
an instant friendship. She shook Melissa's hand rapidly, then
tucked her own into the crook of Surim's arm. "I'm sure Surim
appreciates your working with the Englishman to facilitate the
building of his pet project." She smiled at him. "Do let's move
on—I want to talk to the ambassador."

Surim inclined his head slightly, then turned to escort her to
a small group nearby.

"Beautiful woman," Asid said. "She will make him a fine
wife and give him many sons."

"Always with boys," Melissa grumbled, feeling a tad jealous
as she watched them walk away. She knew there could never
be anything between her and Surim, but earlier he'd kissed her
hand and told her she was beautiful.

Good grief, girl, she told herself, get a grip! She should be
soaking up every moment of this fabulous gathering and not
pining over something that could not be.

"Ah, but Surim needs sons to carry on the ruling of our
country. He was an only child. What would we do if he dies
before he had an heir?"

"Elect someone new," she said.

Hearing the intake of breath at her comment, she looked at Asid and smiled ruefully. "Sorry, western thinking. Let's hope Surim lives many more years and has a dozen sons."

"Perhaps that would be excessive," Asid murmured, his eyes twinkling.

Melissa laughed. "Tell me about your favorite spot in the Lake District," she said.

Asid proved to be entertaining, and Melissa enjoyed their conversation. She was very aware of Surim whenever she spotted him across the room, however, and once stopped mid-sentence to stare when he laughed at something someone had said. It was the first time she'd heard him laugh. His face softened a fraction, lost that austere façade she was used to seeing. And made her heart flip over. She turned so she couldn't see him.

"Would you care to walk in the garden? It grows warm in here," Asid said.

"I should love to. I've been in it a couple of times at night. The lighting makes it easy to walk through and the cooler night air is wonderful to enjoy."

Once away from the crowd, it grew quiet.

"You leave for England in the morning, I believe Surim told me," Asid said as they strolled among the flowers.

"That's right," Melissa said. "I shall be sorry to return to rain and cold after the wonderful climate here. But duty calls."

"You work with Max Valentine, I believe."

"Only temporarily. I'm filling in until my new job starts in February. I'll be going to America then."

"The women in our country are not so well traveled as in England."

Just then a wail sounded from the upper floor.

She turned, searching the windows, seeing a light go on on the top floor.

"Hamid," she said quietly. "Excuse me, Asid. I think I'll go see if I can help. Thanks for your company. I enjoyed myself tremendously. But a little boy needs me."

Without waiting for him to respond, Melissa turned and fled to the house, only slowing her pace to a rapid walk through the gathering of guests, then almost running up the stairs.

The closer she approached the nursery, the louder the screams sounded. She burst into Hamid's bedroom to see Annis standing beside the bed, shaking his shoulder in an attempt to awaken him, speaking in Arabic. Alaya bumped into Melissa, peering into the room.

"He woke me," she complained.

Melissa went to the bed, gently moved Annis aside and sat on the mattress, gathering the little boy into her arms.

"There, there, sweetie, it's all right. Wake up. You're having a nightmare, but you're all right. Wake up, Hamid," she crooned as she rocked him back and forth.

He pushed back a little and quieted down, then snuggled against Melissa. Soon his crying eased.

"Mummy?" he said bewildered.

"No, sweetie, it's Melissa. You're at your cousin Surim's house, remember?"

"I want Mummy," he wailed.

"Shh. Your sister is here and I'm here. You're fine."

"What is going on?" Surim asked from the doorway. Delleah stood beside him, looking around the room, and then at the children.

Annis spoke rapidly in Arabic. Delleah listened avidly.

"Enough," Surim said in English.

"The sooner you send them off to boarding school, the better, Surim," Delleah said.

Hamid stopped crying and looked at Surim.

Alaya turned, stunned. "You're sending us away?" she asked.

Melissa could have slapped Delleah. How cruel of her to make that comment, especially in English. She looked at Surim.

He couldn't send them from this safe haven. They'd lost their home, their parents—he couldn't split them up so they lost each other as well.

"Surim," she began, not sure what she would say, but something to plead for the children.

"I said enough!"

Surim turned to Delleah and spoke to her in Arabic. "I told you that in confidence. Is this how you treat such information?"

She looked stricken. It was well he knew this before their relationship moved any further. Trust was important to him. No matter what Delleah's agenda, and he had a strong suspicion what that was, it did not excuse such a lapse.

"I misspoke. I apologize," she said.

"If you will excuse me, I will deal with my cousins. You may return to the reception. Do not tell anyone of what went on here. Can I trust you this time?" He knew Annis listened, but didn't care. She would be discreet. And his anger was growing that Delleah would deliberately try to force his hand by speaking in English in front of the children.

He was equally aware of Hamid and Alaya drawing closer to Melissa. She held the little boy on her lap now, soothing him. All three stared at him as if he were a stranger.

"As you wish, Surim," Delleah said in a subdued voice. She turned and left without another word.

"What happened?" he asked Annis.

"The boy was screaming, I came in to waken him, but he was sound asleep, screaming. Ayyeee, it was terrible. Then miss came in and spoke to him in English and woke him up."

"You speak English; why didn't you talk to him in that language?"

"My English is not so good. And when I get upset, I forget it," she said, her eyes downcast.

Surim felt his frustration ratchet up another notch. Annis had been his cousin Mara's nanny when she was growing up. And he knew how well Mara had spoken English even before she'd moved to live in England. He had expected her mother to provide the best person for her grandchildren. Maybe three children were too much. Annis had had only Mara when she was growing up. And she'd been much younger.

"You may leave, Annis," he said. "We'll handle this."

Annis bowed slightly and scurried from the room.

He faced Melissa and the children. Only Nadia was missing. He hoped she'd slept through the whole thing.

Melissa spoke in French. "Please reassure these children you are not sending them away. They lost one home already; they can't lose another this soon. Plus, you'll never find a boarding school that would take all three together. Please do not separate them; they need each other as they recover from the loss of their parents."

"And what do you suggest I do instead?" he replied in the same language.

"I don't know. Get someone who speaks English to help them in this transition time."

He stared at her for a long moment. The answer to the situation lay with her. "Very well, I'll let them stay if you stay to care for them."

"What?"

The children looked at her. Melissa knew her voice had gone up several decibels, but the suggestion was preposterous.

"I can't stay here. I have a job waiting in America. I'm starting in a few weeks."

"Stay and help the children adjust," he suggested. "If you're serious about their needing help in the transition. It will also give you time to see more of my country. You would not have total care of them; we have Annis. But you could help them adjust."

Melissa tried to think. It was mid-January. She had a few weeks before she was due in Boston. She could stay until then.

How long would it take for the children to feel more at home? Could they find another English-speaking woman to help with the transition?

What would Max say? She'd committed to working with him until it was time to leave for America. It had been a fill-in job, she knew, but she'd made a commitment.

"Melissa, are we going to be sent away?" Alaya asked.

"No," Melissa said, one look at the children and her mind instantly made up. This was more important. Max would under-stand—she hoped.

She looked at Surim. "I'll stay."

CHAPTER FOUR

MELISSA couldn't believe she'd just committed to staying in Qu'Arim. She was scheduled to return to London in the morning with Max. She still had all her packing to do for her move to America. She'd never in her wildest imagination thought about remaining in Qu'Arim for another two or three weeks.

Max was another problem. She would be leaving him in the lurch if she didn't return. But her mind was made up. Second thoughts weren't going to change it. She couldn't let these sweet children be shuffled off to a boarding school.

"After the children are settled in bed, join me in the study. We'll discuss your stay, and then return to the reception," Surim said formally. With a slight bow, he left.

Alaya watched until he'd gone, then flung her arms around Melissa's neck. "Thank you! We'd love to have you look after us!"

"You're going to be our new mummy?" Hamid asked.

"No, darling, just a temporary visitor." For right now, it looked as if she was staying.

"Let's get some warmed milk with cinnamon and after you drink that you'll be ready to go back to bed with no more nightmares," she said to Hamid.

"Really?" The little boy's lower lip wobbled. "I get so scared. I think a truck is going to crash into me."

"It won't happen, sweetie. The milk will chase away the

nightmares and you'll sleep as good as Nadia," Melissa said, hoping he wouldn't have another this night.

Half an hour later Melissa went back downstairs. The noise level from the voices and the quartet playing in the background rose as she came closer to the ground floor. She looked around, trying to figure out where Surim's study would be located. She knew little about the house except for the third floor and the living room and dining room.

There was an open door down the hall from the reception room, a light shining out. She went toward it.

"Hold a moment, please," a voice called behind her.

Melissa turned. It was Delleah. The woman seemed to glide along as she walked. Her dress was lovely, but her expression was definitely not.

"I'm looking for His Excellency. He asked me to join him in his study," Melissa said. Surely Delleah would know the layout of the house.

"For what purpose?" Delleah asked.

Melissa raised her eyebrows in surprise. "I think that is between us."

Delleah glanced up the stairs. "About those children?"

"It's a private matter," Melissa said, getting annoyed with the woman. If she were so close to Surim, let him answer her questions.

"Private? I thought you just met His Excellency."

"We met on Sunday when Max Valentine and I arrived. If you'll excuse me." Melissa tried to break away without appearing too rude.

"The sooner he gets rid of those children, the better it will be. He is too busy to be encumbered with orphans," Delleah said.

That struck Melissa's hot button. "Their being alone in the world is all the more reason he should pay them attention," she said, quietly but fiercely. "They have recently lost their mother and father. He is their cousin and a link to their parents and he should lavish attention on them until they've recovered from the initial devastation of all they've been through."

Delleah waved a dismissive hand. "A suitable school will do wonders."

"Were you sent away to school?" Melissa asked. What was it with these people that they were so quick to send away the children?

"I was not so fortunate. But many of our children are sent to fine schools. It is not a horrible choice, but enriching," Delleah said. "I plan to send my children to France for schooling. They will get a more cosmopolitan education there then here."

"At age five and two children don't need to be cosmopolitan. Excuse me, I need to find Surim."

"Surim? You know him so well you call him by name?" Delleah clearly didn't like the situation.

Melissa wished she could take back the words. He'd asked her to call him by his name as a friend of Max's. Maybe in public he would wish for more formality. Something she should check on.

"I'll show you the study," Delleah said, walking past Melissa and heading down the hall toward the open door.

Melissa followed her, wondering what the woman was up to. She didn't seem the friendliest person she'd met. And she definitely wasn't Melissa's idea of a good mother. What would her children be like? If she had them with Surim, they'd be gorgeous, Melissa knew that much. But out of sight most of the time?

"Surim, we miss you," Delleah said when she stopped in the doorway. "When your business is finished with the Englishwoman, do rejoin us."

Surim rose from behind a desk, his expression neutral, and crossed to the door. "I would not neglect my guests except for matters of utmost importance. I'll be there shortly. Melissa, please come in. Delleah, if you'll excuse us."

He shut the door behind Melissa, almost in Delleah's face.

"Come and sit," Surim invited, motioning to the comfortable chairs near the windows. The faint illumination from the gardens cast a warm light on the shrubs and flowers visible through the tall windows.

Melissa sat and waited, her nerves on edge.

"I will speak to Max, if you like," Surim offered, sitting in the chair near hers.

"I'll tell him. As soon as we finalize arrangements. I can still do the translations from here, if he wishes, and if you will permit. I hate to leave a job in the middle of it," she said, hoping it would be agreeable with both men. Even if she had to do it after the children were in bed at night, she'd be able to keep up. Most of the plans had been finalized this week, so Melissa didn't expect a lot of translations in the next few weeks.

"I have committed to a new post in mid-February, however," she said.

"Cancel it," Surim ordered.

Melissa blinked. "No, I am quite looking forward to it. Besides, that gives me almost a month to get the children settled."

He leaned back and steepled his hands, resting his chin on his fingertips. "Annis was the children's mother's nurse. She's a generation removed now, but longs to raise these children. I hope working together you two can make a difference with the children."

"I'll do my best."

"And if they are not settled by the time your next commitment comes?"

"I'm sure you could find someone. Who wouldn't wish to work here? The accommodations are lovely. I think women will be falling all over themselves for the assignment."

"Yet you are not," he commented.

"I have a position lined up." For a second Melissa wondered if she should reconsider. Granted, she'd told the McDonalds she'd be there when their current nanny married, but Qu'Arim was nothing like Boston. If she extended her stay, she'd have the tropical setting to enjoy all year instead of living in months of winter each year. She already knew these children. She remembered the McDonald children; they'd stayed for two weeks. But they didn't need her as much as the three upstairs did.

Not that Surim had offered her the nanny's position. That stayed with Annis. She would stay to help out Max's friend, then head for Boston.

He studied her for a moment. Melissa pushed away her doubts. She could help for a short time. Though she knew if she wanted a shot at getting any concessions, now was the time, before he took her for granted.

"There are a couple of conditions to my staying," she said slowly, testing his reaction.

Surim continued to stare at her. She wished she knew what he was thinking.

Lowering his hands, he inclined his head slightly. "And those are?" No telling his thoughts from his voice.

"More involvement from you, for starters," she said audaciously. It was so important for him to spend time getting to know these children. Nannies were employees after all. And she was a stranger. Much as she loved working with children, they weren't her family or Annis's. These children were Surim's now.

That seemed to surprise him. "I lead a very busy life."

She nodded. "I'm sure, but you are in charge of that life. Carve out some time to spend with your children."

"They are not—"

Melissa raised a hand, knowing if she survived this interview, it would be a miracle. But she didn't care. She was fighting for those precious children upstairs.

"They are not your biological children, granted, but they are now your kids. You are their guardian, which makes you their parental figure. You'll have more influence on their lives than anyone else. I think it's important you get to know them, and let them get to know you."

"They are afraid of me," he said slowly.

"They don't know you. I think they're shy, scared and unhappy. And your announcement tonight about sending them away didn't help."

"It was not my announcement," he retorted.

Melissa waved her hand as if brushing the comment away.

"And your other demands?"

"They don't get on well with Annis. Something should be worked out to make sure they can get along better before the children become too resentful. I think Annis is a bit over-whelmed—sad herself over the death of their mother. But they need to work together."

"Agreed. Suggestions?" he asked.

"I thought she could start teaching them Arabic. And have them teach her more English. Give them both a place, and help bridge the differences."

"Easily handled. Is that it?" he asked.

"One more thing. I think it's very important that they eat with you as family at least once or twice a week. Which will foster company manners, and get them used to their position in their society when they are older."

"A two-year-old at dinner? Will she dress?" The sarcasm was unmistakable.

Melissa held her ground. "I'll see about that. Maybe she should start at age three or four. But Hamid and Alaya are old enough. This is their culture, their history, their family. They will get their family values and traditions from you. It's important"

Surim nodded.

"And you would join us. Perhaps even get Annis to teach you some Arabic."

"I would like to, though I won't be here long enough to learn much. Still, it's a good idea; I can learn with them."

"Any other conditions?" he asked.

"No. Shall I get a uniform?"

He looked startled. "You are not an employee; you would remain my guest while you are here. I hope you'll have time to see more of Qu'Arim and enjoy yourself as well as help me out with the children."

"Oh." She hadn't expected that. She'd thought she'd be a sub-nanny or something. This changed things. For a moment the warmth of his kiss flashed through her mind. She was to remain a guest!

"Would that be a hardship?"

She smiled and shook her head. "Of course not; I had thought it a job."

"No. So, when I'm home, I will hope you will join me for meals. You can give me an update on their progress. And be the buffer between us on the nights they dine with us."

Melissa felt a surge of excitement. She would make the most of her weeks as a guest and see as much of the country as she could. Maybe Surim would take her—

He rose. "If that is all, I should return to my guests."

Melissa stood as well. She was a foolish woman if she thought this busy man would take time to show her the countryside. She admonished herself not to let her daydreams carry her away.

"I'll find Max and let him know I'm not returning home with him in the morning," she said, wondering if he would advise against her staying.

The sheikh escorted her back to the reception room. Delleah stood near the doorway, talking with friends and keeping her eyes on the door.

Melissa scarcely noticed as she entered and began to search for Max. She saw him near the opened French doors, in deep discussion with several men. Feeling a bit self-conscious, Melissa walked to the group, hoping to catch Max's eye and get him alone for a moment or two. She felt as if she were on a tilt-a-wheel: one moment she was a translator preparing to leave, now she was a guest of the sheikh's, staying for several weeks.

Max noticed her and excused himself from the group to join Melissa. "Something up?" he asked.

"Change in plans. The sheikh asked me to stay a little longer, to help with getting the children used to living here."

"What do you mean?"

She explained. Ending with, "Do you think I'm doing the right thing? And what about your translations? Could I do them from here and fax you the English?"

Max thought carefully before answering. "Melissa, you're the only one who can decide if it's the right thing. But you'll have a chance to see more of the country, unless I miss my guess. Surim's a wonderful host. But will you spend too much time with the children to do translations?"

"I don't think so. It's not as if I'm in charge of them. I'll do whatever is needed from here and fax you the results. That way there won't be any delays. It's been working that you got the faxed documents and I translated. Now, I'll just translate first. It's only for a few weeks. You know I start my new job in America in mid-February."

"Does Surim know?"

"I told him. If it looks as if the children aren't getting settled, he'll have plenty of time to find another qualified woman to help. It beats his other idea of shipping them off to some boarding school. Nadia is only two!"

"Well, if you're sure," Max said, concern creasing his forehead.

Melissa was anything but sure she was making a good decision. But the thought of the children wiped all doubts from her mind. She knew she could help get them acclimated to their new circumstances.

The party lost some of its luster for her as she began to catalog all the things she needed to do. Not sure she'd see Max in the morning before she left, she asked him to reassure her mother. She'd contact her in the morning. She found Asid ibn Tarvor to thank him for his courtesies and then left the reception to return to her room. It was late and she had things to think about. But her last thoughts, just before she drifted off to sleep, were of Surim.

Melissa awoke early the next morning, and quickly donned a skirt and blouse. She'd have to call her mother today to tell her the change in plans and to ask her to send some clothes. The outfits she'd brought were much more suitable to an office than spending time with children.

Once dressed, she quickly went upstairs. Hamid and Nadia were quietly playing in the nursery. The table was set for breakfast, but the food hadn't arrived. Nadia saw her first.

"Melissa!" She jumped up and ran to her. "Are you going to eat with us?"

Hamid rose and came over. "Are you really staying like you said last night?"

"I am to both. We'll have breakfast first, then plan our week. Where's Alaya?"

"She's still sleeping," Hamid said. "Shall I go and wake her up?"

Annis came into the room and looked surprised to see Melissa. "Did you come to see the children?" She looked around, noticing Alaya was absent.

"Actually, I came to have breakfast with them," Melissa said. Had no one told her of the change in plans?

"I will see the kitchen sends up more food," Annis said, clearly puzzled. "I hope we will not delay your departure."

"I think His Excellency needs to discuss things with you," Melissa said carefully, not wanting to offend Annis. "I'm staying for a few weeks to help with the children. I hope that together we can make the transition easier for them. It's hard losing their parents and then their home, and it will take a while before this feels like home for them."

"Are you really staying?" Alaya asked from the doorway. She was already dressed in shorts and a top and wore sandals. She smiled hopefully at Melissa.

"Just for a little while. I have to leave for America in February."

"We want you to stay forever," Hamid said enthusiastically.

Melissa smiled and tousled his hair. "I'll be here for a long visit. I shall love spending time with all three of you. You'll have to tell me all you know about Qu'Arim. Maybe we can go exploring." She loved seeing the children's delighted faces. "First, though, let's eat and then we'll make plans."

It was the middle of the school year at home, and Melissa suspected the children had had little schooling since their arrival. Not that she would have expected them to work over the Christmas holidays, but it was January, time to get back into a routine. She'd ask Annis what provisions had been made for their education. Nadia was far too young for lessons, except the fun kind that would teach her colors, shapes and numbers. Would the sheikh hire a governess or tutor? Once they knew enough Arabic, they could attend the local schools.

The three children were delighted with Melissa's company. Breakfast was enjoyable, and each ate everything on their plate. Annis did not remain, but left as soon as the meal had been served from the kitchen. Melissa hoped her feelings weren't hurt. She had to get her involved as she would be the one with them after Melissa left.

By four o'clock, the younger children were up from naps. Alaya had read a good portion of a new book while they slept. Now it was time for fun. Melissa had them get ready to go for a short swim. She wanted to assess the abilities of the children and get them into the fresh air and sunshine. They'd been patient all day while she and Annis had discussed their care and education. Melissa hoped the swim would be reward enough.

"For you, Miss Fox." One of the liveried servants brought an envelope on a small silver tray.

Feeling like the lady of the manor, Melissa took it and opened it.

'Max safely on his way. I am tied up and will be unable to be home for dinner.' It was signed 'Surim'.

She studied the bold script for a long moment, feeling a free-fall sensation in her stomach. She was disappointed. She'd hoped to see him today. That was obviously out of the question.

Still she stared at the note. She'd been very careful not to call him by name since Delleah had noticed. Not wishing to presume on his relationship with her new stepbrother, she'd kept their brief contact formal.

Now he signed the note with his name. Could she continue to call him Surim? Or keep the more formal title?

With a sigh, she folded the paper and put it in her pocket. Nothing she had to decide today.

By the time the children were in bed that night, Melissa was tired enough to go to bed herself. Thinking a quick walk in the gardens would refresh her, she slipped out from the opened French doors in the living room.

The day had gone well. Annis had been happy to learn Melissa was staying for a few weeks with the sole goal of helping the children adjust. She had been pleased when Melissa had asked her to teach them all Arabic.

"Enough for the children to be able to communicate on a basic level. Reading and writing can wait for school, though I suspect Hamid and Nadia will find it easier if they start school knowing basics. Alaya is already reading English and writing compositions. I expect learning Arabic will be more difficult for her."

"Do they wish to learn?" Annis asked, clearly puzzled.

"This will be their home, won't it? They need to speak the language. Who better to teach them? I understand you were the children's mother's nanny. They would so love to hear about her when she was growing up. You can practice Arabic with them when telling them of her childhood."

"We do not speak of her," Annis had said.

"Why ever not?"

Annis seemed to hesitate, frowning. "So not to remind the children of their loss."

"It would be good for the children to hear as much about their parents as they can, to keep them alive in their memory and so they'll know others remember them fondly. With love," explained Melissa gently. "I hope to arrange a visit with their grandmother to see pictures of their mother when she was younger."

Annis nodded. "There were many. I have some myself. Mara was such a special child."

"Then share that memory with her children. You'll find they will respond positively."

By the time she relaxed in the twilight, Melissa felt better than she had all day. This temporary stay would work out perfectly. She loved working with the children. She just hoped Surim would find time in his schedule to spend with them. He wouldn't be able to help falling in love with them.

"I see you have found a favorite spot of mine," a voice said.

Startled, Melissa smiled when Surim stepped from the darkness into the subdued light from the garden path. "I love your gardens. You know the English—we are always growing flowers. This garden is beautiful."

"I do not claim credit," he said, sitting beside her on the bench. "I have excellent gardeners who take care of that. The fragrances are a delight to the senses, as are the colors and designs of the plants."

"A haven," she murmured, acutely aware of him so close.

Now her heart was starting to race. She had better become immune to his charm or she was in serious trouble.

"Exactly." He was silent for a moment. "I have another."

"Another what?"

"Haven. It's in the desert, isolated, wild, beautiful. A small oasis deep in the interior. From time to time I go there to remember where our people came from. The hectic modern life is inevitable, but we were a nomadic people, calling the desert home. I like to return to remember."

"I bet it's beautiful."

"Some find it so. Others find it stark and unappealing."

Melissa sighed, imagining the scene. "I should love to see some of the desert. Your capital is as modern as London. And doesn't feel much different, except for the signs in Arabic. But to visit the desert, that would be quite different."

He smiled. She caught her breath and looked away before she did something idiotic.

"Perhaps we'll find time before you leave."

"I should enjoy that," she said primly, belying the joy that flared at the prospect. Then she turned to face him.

"Do you normally return home from work so late?" she asked. She knew running a country was a bit different from a job in banking, but these hours seemed a bit excessive.

"Tonight was another business dinner, with much negotiations and posturing. The ancient protocols are wearing."

"You're the man in charge—change them," she said flippantly. Being near him upset her sense of balance. She could stare at the man for hours, and probably find something new at each second. Like the few gray strands at his temples. He was too young to be going gray. Probably the stress of his position.

"How were the children?" he asked. "Run you ragged yet?"

"After one day? Hardly. They have lots of energy; the secret is to channel it and let it run. We made progress, I think. They like the beach. And Annis was a bit more relaxed around them today."

"Now they are in bed."

"Of course, and have been for more than a couple of hours. I need to check on them. Care to join me?"

He rose and nodded. As the light shone on his face Melissa saw the fatigue. It was not her place to make personal comments, but she thought he could use a good night's sleep. She hoped Hamid wouldn't disrupt that tonight.

Annis was still sitting in the nursery, crocheting. She rose when Surim entered, but he motioned her to resume her seat.

"All is well?" he asked in Arabic.

"They sleep. After the running around they did today, I expect they won't wake until morning," she replied. With a glance at Melissa, she continued, "Miss wishes for me to teach them Arabic."

"A good idea. Even if they don't remain here all their lives, they are from this country; it is appropriate that they learn our language and our customs. You would do well to teach them."

"She wishes to learn as well," Annis added.

"Is that a problem?"

"No. Will she be staying long?"

"I have hopes she will stay until the children are settled. She has other commitments in February. Do you think she is helping?"

"Yes. They were easier to deal with today. Maybe she could stay longer?"

"It is too early to say, but I also hope she will stay longer." He turned to look at Melissa, knowing she'd have something to say to his plans if she knew of them.

Melissa had crossed to the doorway to Hamid's room, pausing for a moment before entering. Surim followed in time to see her cover the little boy with a light blanket.

Hamid stirred. "Mummy?" he said, half asleep.

"No, darling. Mummy is in heaven. It's Melissa. You're safe. You'll always be safe here." She patted his arm gently. Hamid snuggled down and went back to sleep.

When she turned, she saw Surim.

"He's afraid, that's why he has nightmares. He misses his parents, but the nightmares are of a truck smashing into him."

"As the truck did his parents," Surim said, his face in shadow.

Melissa nodded. "As he imagines it. I think he will gradually get over this stage. But it may take a while."

"So we can expect more screams in the night," Surim said.

"Not expect, but maybe not be surprised by them," she said. "But I'm hoping with a regime of lessons and outdoor activities, they'll all be so tired at night, they'll sleep through. They are so fortunate to be here where the weather is conducive to playing outside. At home it's cold and rainy."

"We get our share of rain. But rarely does it get cold. If you need anything for the children, ask Annis. She'll get it for you."

"Tomorrow, you'll spend some time with them?"

Surim glanced at Hamid. He couldn't remember being that young. What did a grown man talk to a small child about?

"I have a meeting at ten."

"On Saturday? At least have breakfast with them," Melissa suggested. "We can eat at eight, and finish in plenty of time."

Surim nodded. "I'll see about breakfast. You will be there as well."

"Of course. If you have no time tomorrow, how about Sunday? You could come to the beach with us. The children love the water and playing on the sand. There are a lot of activities that include all three, despite the difference in their ages."

Surim mentally sorted through the things he'd planned for Sunday. Discarding them, he agreed. It was worth it, he decided a moment later, when Melissa gave him a delighted smile. He knew he stared longer than necessary, but her expressions fascinated him. Her smile was open and joyful. He suspected she didn't have a clue how to dissemble or hide her feelings. She was different from most of the women he knew. Maybe he'd take the time to get to know her better and find a way to get her to stay.

CHAPTER FIVE

PROMPTLY at eight the next morning Melissa arrived at the nursery. The children were already dressed and playing a game of keep away, with little Nadia the one in the middle. They greeted Melissa and ran over to her. Nadia lifted her arms to be picked up. Melissa scooped her up, hugged her and then held her as she greeted the other children.

"We're so hungry. Once you arrived, Annis said we could eat," Alaya said.

The table had been set for four, but there was ample room to add place settings. Melissa called to Annis.

"Good morning," the older woman said as she entered. She looked at the children, then back at Melissa. "Is there something wrong?"

"We'll need another place setting at the table," Melissa said. "Do we have the utensils here, or do we need to call down to the kitchen?"

"There are additional settings in the cupboard," Annis indicated. "But why? I will take a tray in my room. You eat with the children."

"His Excellency will be joining us."

"Who?" Hamid asked.

"Your uncle Surim," Melissa said. She put Nadia down and went to the cupboard.

There was whispering behind her. She gathered what she needed and turned to see the three children aligned together, a mutinous look on their respective faces.

"We don't want him here," Alaya said.

"He doesn't like us, so we don't like him," Hamid added.

"Nonsense," Melissa said, returning to the table and quickly setting an additional place. "You all just need to get to know one another."

"He wants to send us away," Alaya said.

"Can we come live with you?" Hamid asked.

"Oh, sweetie, I don't have a place of my own. Besides, I'm sure that would never be allowed. Let's do our best to get to know him. He may surprise you." Melissa hoped so. From what she'd seen thus far, Surim was much more suited in the seat of power than in the nursery. She hoped she'd be surprised.

He arrived a few minutes later. Formally greeting each child, he turned to her and raised an eyebrow, as if asking if she was happy with his presence.

"Good morning. We're glad you could join us," Melissa said. She couldn't help being slightly amused at his expression. Honestly, what would it take to get him to relax?

"No, we're not," Hamid muttered, scowling.

Surim's eyes met hers in amusement as he heard Hamid's comment. "So we eat? I do have a meeting at ten I can't be late to."

"We'll be finished long before then," she assured him.

They sat at the table, Surim at one end, Melissa at the other, with Alaya next to her and Nadia beyond. Hamid sat on the other side. Almost like a family, Melissa thought as she began to serve the English breakfast the kitchen supplied to the children. She gave a heaping portion to Surim, smaller portions to the children. The milk had been poured. The carafe of hot coffee was near Surim's place. Melissa wondered for a moment if he would pour his own, or did he expect her to jump up to serve him?

To her relief, he poured a cup and offered her the carafe. She declined, preferring tea.

"So what are your plans for the day?" Surim asked her.

"Children, what are we doing today?" Melissa asked, hoping to involve them in the conversation, wishing Surim had asked them, not her.

Silence met her question; all three looked at her with entreaty in their eyes.

"Nadia?" she prompted.

"Going to the beach," she said quietly.

"Right." Melissa smiled, wishing something would break the silence. "And what's your favorite part of the beach, Hamid?"

He stared at his plate. "Swimming," he said.

Exasperated, Melissa glanced at Surim. He was calmly eating. She couldn't give a guess to his feelings; his expression was totally impassive.

"Alaya, did you finish your letters to your friends? Maybe Uncle Surim could post them on his way into work today?"

"Why does he have to work on Saturday?" Alaya asked Melissa.

"Ask him, why don't you?"

The child hesitated, then turned to face Surim. "Why do you work on Saturday? My father didn't. He spent Saturdays with Mummy and us. I thought unless you work in a shop or something, Saturdays and Sundays were for family."

"Some things don't wait. There will be other Saturdays when we can spend the day together. What would you like to do if I didn't have to work?"

Alaya shrugged. "Nothing special. Going to the beach is nice. Especially in January." She turned back to Melissa. "I told my friends that in the letter. They'll be so envious."

"I worked in Switzerland before coming here. And there's lots of snow there now. I much prefer warmer climates!" Melissa said, smiling at the girl.

"I'd rather be home," Hamid muttered.

"This is your home, now," Surim said.

"No, it's not. And you want to send us away," Hamid replied, glaring at Surim.

"I want to go home," Nadia said. She pushed away her plate and knocked her milk glass, sending a cascade of white liquid off the table and right into Surim's lap.

For a stunned moment, no one moved. All three children looked at Surim in horror. Nadia's eyes filled with tears.

"I sorry." She began to cry.

"No sense crying over spilt milk," Melissa said calmly, jumping up to go to the child. She handed Surim another napkin and swept Nadia up into her arms. "Don't cry, sweetie, we all know it was an accident. No harm done."

She glanced at Surim. His suit definitely needed a cleaning before he could wear it in public. How he reacted to this mishap would give her the best clue as to how he was going to deal with the children. She hoped he wouldn't get angry over the two-year-old's accident.

He didn't. Slowly he rose, blotting the liquid from the trousers.

"It appears I need to change before I leave for my meeting." With that, he turned and left.

Nadia hugged Melissa. "It accident," she said.

"Of course it was, sweetie. Uncle Surim knows that. He wasn't even mad."

"Yes, he was," Hamid said. "Now he'll send us away for sure. What if we can't all go to the same school?"

For a moment Melissa thought he was going to start crying as well.

"He's not sending you away. I'm here to make sure that doesn't happen. His inviting me to stay doesn't sound like someone sending you away. Now finish eating or you won't have enough energy to play at the beach.

She resettled the children and the meal passed without further mishap.

Once finished, she asked Annis to watch them for a moment and dashed down the stairs, hoping to find Surim before he left.

When she reached the ground floor, she looked around. No sign of him, but she didn't expect him to be hanging around the foyer. She walked down the hall to the study. The door was open and he was standing by his desk, putting folders into his briefcase.

"Do you have a moment?" Melissa asked.

He turned and nodded. "But only a minute. I need to leave soon."

"I know. I wanted to apologize for the mishap this morning. She's only two."

"Am I such an ogre I can't recognize a child's accident?"

"I'm not saying you are, but you have to admit you don't have a lot of experience around children."

"Perhaps it would be better to wait until they are older before taking our meals together," he said, turning back to the briefcase.

Melissa stepped into the room. She was beginning to get a bit annoyed with the refrain.

"It's never too early for children to be part of a family, especially at meals. They were nervous. They'll do better when they get used to you."

"They don't like me," he said calmly. "I heard them from the hall."

For a stunned moment Melissa wondered if their careless comments had actually hurt Surim. She dismissed it. He was an adult; he knew children said things in the heat of the moment. But for a moment she wanted to reach out and reassure him.

"They don't *know* you," she said. "Remember back when you were little. You wanted to be grown up and do things with adults. But it was hard."

"I do not remember back when I was two," he said.

"Then use your imagination!"

He closed his case and looked at her.

"They are well cared for, have everything they could need."

"No, they don't. They need love. They need someone who is interested in them, in what they are doing, what they think, what they are learning."

"You're there for that."

"Not for long! They need family."

Surim took a moment to consider her passionate statement. She hardly knew the children upstairs, yet she was definitely their advocate. He liked the way she flared up in their defense. Her eyes sparkled, color flooded her cheeks. She had passion and determination. For a moment he was struck with how beautiful she looked. Would she flare in passion for the right man? What would Melissa look like in bed?

He looked away, not liking his thoughts. Too often over the last few days he'd caught himself thinking about his guest. She was leaving in a few weeks. Maybe asking her to stay had been a mistake.

For a moment, he tried to imagine being two and having just lost his parents. He'd been spared that. His parents hadn't died until he was seventeen. Not that they had spent much time with him. He'd gone off to school in England at age nine. He'd been lonely and homesick, but had hidden the fact from the world. Outwardly, he'd projected an image of self-sufficiency. Internally, he'd been a small boy longing for home and parents. Remembering would help him empathize with the children.

"I don't know how to make them feel wanted," he said slowly. He knew how to run his country, after years of trial and error; years of frustration and triumphs. But he didn't know how to relate to a two-year-old girl. He wasn't someone used to failure. Somehow, he had to learn to relate to them.

And focus on them. Not on the temporary guest who would be leaving in February.

Melissa nodded. "The only suggestion I can make is to spend more time with them. Today would have been good going to the beach. Can you join us later? Nadia naps after lunch, while the others play quietly. But we could go back after that."

The last thing Surim had expected when he'd awoken this morning was to cancel plans to take an excursion to the beach. He didn't have time to rearrange his entire schedule to deal with three children.

Yet they were Mara's children. And if he didn't get to know them now, then when?

"If I can arrange it, I'll join you." He'd have to call Delleah and cancel their plans for dinner. Not that it would be a hardship. He knew she had hopes of marriage, but after the way she'd betrayed his confidence he'd had second thoughts.

She had seemed suitable. Yet there were many suitable women available. It would be best to make haste slowly, as his teacher in England had often said.

"One more thing before you go. Can we arrange a time to take them to see their grandmother? I think that would help with the transition. I know you said she's in frail health, but a short visit would be all right, wouldn't it?" she asked.

"I will call and make arrangements."

"That would be perfect. I'll coach them on manners and hope she doesn't offer milk and biscuits in the drawing room," Melissa said, teasing.

He looked away before he forgot she was a guest in his home and reached out to kiss her. Her mouth was eminently kissable.

"She does speak English, doesn't she?" Melissa asked.

"Yes, quite well. She visited the children in England. Since the death of her daughter, however, she's been prostrate with grief and has not made an effort to see them. I will make sure she does so."

"Maybe I had better not tell them until you confirm. I don't want to raise hopes to have them dashed down."

Surim nodded. "I will have my secretary call once we've confirmed the visit. Now, if you would excuse me, I do have to get to that meeting." he said. But even as he spoke, for the first time since he could remember, he didn't want to deal with affairs of state. Maybe he should arrange that trip to the oasis with Melissa. Yet he hesitated. How involved with the English guest did he wish to become? He had not shared his desert retreat with anyone.

She nodded and turned to leave. Surim followed her to the foyer. Melissa intrigued him. She was the only woman he knew that didn't flirt. At least not with him. She was more concerned for three children she scarcely knew.

Was his interest in her merely because of that? Perhaps he was getting spoiled with the attention normally received and was annoyed she also didn't seem to fall in line.

Wouldn't Max laugh if he knew his thoughts?

Once in the car a few moments later, Surim reviewed his schedule for the next few days. With some juggling of appointments, some more delegation of duties, he might be able to free up a few days to spend with his guest. She was doing him a favor in helping with the children. The least he could do was make sure she saw more of the country—and didn't spend her entire visit with the under-ten set.

It was shortly after four when Surim strode onto the beach. The meetings had ended shortly after one, but he'd spent the rest of the afternoon trying to rearrange his schedule. He paused a moment watching the scene. Alaya was splashing in the water, laughing. From this distance he could see back across the years to when he and Mara had played in the sea. They'd been fearless—diving, swimming, racing. How she'd loved the water.

Hamid was building another sandcastle. This one was almost as tall as he was. Surim suspected he'd had some help from Melissa. But at the moment she was occupied with Nadia. He wasn't sure what they were doing, but it looked as if they were making building blocks from wet sand. Too small to be for Hamid's castle. Perhaps they planned one of their own.

Melissa noticed him first. Her look of delight jolted something inside him. For a moment, Surim wanted to simply bask in the bright smile she gave so frequently. She was wearing shorts and her legs looked golden against the sand. Her laughter rang out and he soaked it in. He trusted her in a way he didn't often trust. Was it because Max vouched for her? Or her own innate sense of fair play that appealed to him?

She must have told Nadia he had arrived because the little girl looked over. Gravely she rose and started toward him.

He walked to meet her, noticing the other children had seen him as well.

"Hi, Uncle Surim," Nadia said simply, raising her arms to be picked up.

He lifted her, surprised at how little she weighed. "Are you enjoying yourself at the beach?" he asked. What did one say to a two-year-old?

"Yes. Me and Lissa are making cakes. Do you want one?"

Use your imagination, Melissa had told him. He smiled at the little girl. "I'd very much love to try one of your cakes."

"Only pretend, don't really put in your mouth," she said.

"I can do that." He'd reached the castle. "Good job, Hamid," he said, studying the structure. It was surprisingly complex for so young a child.

Hamid smiled, not meeting Surim's eyes, but he could tell the boy was pleased with the praise.

"Alaya, not so far out," Melissa called. Surim turned to look at the child in the water just as Alaya turned and swam back toward shore.

"She swims well, like her mother," Surim said joining Melissa.

"And she wants to swim farther out in the deeper water, but I can't watch her closely and the other two as well. If she gets in trouble, I don't want her so far out it would take long to rescue her."

"I will swim with her. Her mother and I loved to race to the buoy."

Melissa looked at the marker bobbing in the water some distance away.

"That far?" she asked doubtfully.

"We were a little older, but not much. Mara loved the water."

"So do her children." Melissa smiled at him holding the toddler. "I see you and Nadia have made up."

"Nothing to make up. It was an accident."

"Your suit was ruined."

"Milk-stained only. A competent cleaner will get it back to normal. And if not, it's only a suit. I have plenty."

"Want me to take her?" Melissa held out her arms for Nadia, but the little girl threw her arms around Surim's neck.

"No, we have cake," she said.

"I said I'd try one, but it's only pretend, I can't eat it," Surim said.

Melissa nodded. "Very good, Nadia. I've been telling her that all day. I think she believes the sand is sugar. It does look like it, though, so white and fine."

While Surim sat with Nadia and played they were eating cake, Melissa glanced around. Hamid was settled, Alaya not too distant.

"Melissa, come and swim," Alaya called. She stood waist-deep in the blue water, beckoning.

"Why don't you go swim with her now?" Melissa suggested. "Tell her about racing with her mother."

Surim nodded. "Do you want to go swimming too?" he asked Nadia.

The little girl nodded.

"I'll take her for a short swim, then bring her right back and go with Alaya," he said. In only a moment he'd set the toddler down to remove his shirt and shorts.

Melissa caught her breath at the sight of his bare chest. It was the warm color of teak, solid and muscular. She was surprised at how fit he was. Business suits hid all that. And a good thing, she thought, forcing her gaze away. She clenched her hands into fists, feeling the grit of the sand. Better than giving into temptation to trace the contours of those muscles. Feel the warmth of his skin.

Get a grip, she admonished. If Surim ever caught a hint of her attraction, he'd send her packing so fast her head would spin. Then what of the children?

Of course, leaving might be the best thing. She knew she would be a total idiot to fall for him. The sooner he established a relationship with these children, the better.

"Are you all right?" he asked.

Melissa nodded, scrambling to her feet. "I'll see if Hamid wishes to go swimming now," she said, refusing to let her eyes feast on that tanned expanse before her. She'd seen men swimming before, for heaven's sake. Ignore him, she told her roiling senses.

The remainder of the afternoon passed swiftly. Melissa kept a prudent distance from her host. The children were cautious in their approach to Surim, but by the end of the swimming race Alaya was laughing and seemed comfortable around her much older cousin.

Surim excused himself as they headed back for the house, claiming a prior engagement. Melissa was just as glad not to test the children's manners at dinner; they were too tired after their exertions to behave without being cranky.

Melissa was also glad to escape the presence of Surim for personal reasons. She was stunned at the attraction that grew the longer she was around him. She'd be leaving soon. And even if she wasn't, she would never succumb to the cliché of falling for the dashing man. Sheikh Surim Al-Thani could look at whomever he wanted for his bride. The last person he'd consider falling for was a children's nanny.

Besides, after thinking herself in love with Paul Hemrich, and having that end disastrously, the last thing she needed was to fall for a man so far from her realm. She'd gotten over the heartache of Paul during the last few months. But she was still feeling a bit bruised and had no wish to repeat that experience!

Once the children were in bed, Melissa retired to her room. She'd write to her mother and to some friends in Switzerland, and forget about Paul. And Surim.

However, Melissa found it was easy to forget the young German banker she'd found so fascinating, but a different matter to refrain from thinking about her host. Recalling the beautiful, sultry beauty she'd met at the reception, Melissa knew she didn't stand a chance, even if their circumstances had been different.

Sighing softly, she resumed her letters, trying to keep focused on them.

Try as she might, however, her letters related a lot about Surim, from working with him on the restaurant project, to his difficulty associating with the children, to the attempts he was making at forging family ties.

Throwing down her pen a little later, she rose and stretched. She'd reread the pages in the morning and then ask to have them posted. In the meantime, she herself was tired from the day in the sunshine. Was Surim still out at his prior engagement? Was it dinner with the beautiful Delleah? Would he be asking her to marry him at that very moment?

Frowning, Melissa hoped not. Delleah didn't seem to like the children. How would that work to have her become their stepmother?

Before going to bed, she'd love a hot cup of tea. Wondering if she could just zip into the kitchen and make herself a pot without bothering anyone, she left her room and headed for the dining room. From there she'd be able to locate the kitchen, she hoped.

She'd barely stepped foot on the ground floor before one of Surim's servants stepped out of the shadows.

"Do you wish something?" he asked in French.

"Some tea, please," she replied.

"I'm happy to get it for you. Please wait in the drawing room." He vanished into the darkened hallway.

"So much for a midnight kitchen raid," she murmured, walking into the still-lighted formal drawing room. It was decorated with exotic heavy furnishings, some pieces quite old. She loved the richness of the colors of the fabrics, the deep maroons, peacock-blues and iridescent greens. Brass tacks outlined several chair arms. On the walls were magnificent paintings, huge landscapes of the desert and some of the beautiful blue Persian Gulf. There were displays of pearls in one cabinet. She crossed the room to study them. Maybe she could get a tour at one of the pearl farms before she left Qu'Arim.

The display was fabulous. She wished she knew more about pearls. The color variation was amazing, from snowy white to deep cream even to one which was a dark, shimmering gray. A couple were the size of her thumb, but most were much smaller. Perfect spheres, they were displayed on satin that captured their sheen and enhanced the color.

"Beautiful, aren't they?" Surim asked from the doorway.

Melissa turned, surprised. "Oh, yes, they are. I wondered if I might be able to see the divers one day before I leave."

"I'm sure a visit can be arranged to one of the beds, but the pearl season is summer, not winter, so there would be little to see. You're up late."

"I'm waiting for a cup of tea. I thought I might just dash down to get it for myself, but one of your servants met me in the hall and asked me to wait here while he went for it. I didn't mean to cause any trouble."

"It is our pleasure to look after our guests," Surim said. "The more welcomed we make you feel, the longer you will stay."

She smiled wistfully. "It would be lovely to do so. I'll hate leaving this warm climate for snow and ice. But I've already accepted and it wouldn't be fair to the McDonalds to back out at the last minute. I know their children. They're counting on me. Besides, I can't stay on indefinitely. That would be taking hospitality too far."

"It would be my pleasure."

Melissa shook her head. "Thank you for asking, but I have to stand by my commitment."

He studied her for a moment, then inclined his head slightly. "The offer remains open should you change your mind."

The servant entered carrying a tray with a teapot and two cups. He placed them on the table in front of the sofa and bowed before leaving.

"Enough for two?" Surim asked.

"So it seems. Would you like some?"

"I should be delighted to join you."

He waited until she sat on the sofa, then took a seat on the chair next to it. Melissa poured the fragrant beverage into two cups, handing him one. His fingertips brushed hers when he took the cup.

"I may have some more documents for you to translate for Max tomorrow. I'll have them brought to the house," Surim said. "We discussed further enhancements tonight at dinner and I want to make sure they meet Max's approval. He's very protective of this new venture."

"Oh, I thought—" Melissa started, then quickly took a sip of tea.

"Thought what?" Surim asked.

"That your engagement tonight was personal."

"A date?" he asked calmly.

She nodded.

"It was a meeting with the contractor. The changes need to be incorporated early, so there was no time for delay. As I said, I consider you a guest in my house. I would include you in social events."

Melissa looked surprised. "I understood you are looking for a wife. I'd hardly expect to be included when you and a date are having dinner."

"Ah, but we don't need privacy if I have dinner with someone. In Qu'Arim we don't view marriage the same as you do in England. Here it is primarily an alliance between two families."

"Arranged marriages?"

"For the most part. Parents arrange the marriage settlement. Powerful families are allied with other powerful families, or the arrangements supplement areas of weakness within different families. Maybe one is strong in commerce while another is strong in transportation, a perfect mix."

"What about love?"

"One always hopes affection will grow from the union," Surim said.

"So no one marries for love? What about the children's parents?"

"As it happens, they had known each other as children and had fallen in love. Their parents settled the terms of the marriage, but for them it was the best of both our customs and western custom."

"So you're not looking for love in a match?" Melissa thought that sounded rather cold. She couldn't imagine being married and not being passionately in love with her husband.

Surim sipped his tea, regarding her over the rim of the cup. Setting it back on the saucer and placing both on the table, he sat back in the chair. "It's a western belief. I shall find a suitable woman."

"Sounds sad to me. Where would be the joy?" Melissa asked.

"I would choose someone who had similar interests; we would be compatible in that regard. And find happiness in children."

"You have three children—so far it doesn't look as if they're bringing you a lot of happiness," she commented dryly. If she hadn't stepped in, they would be on their way to a boarding school hundreds of miles away.

"You are correct. I will admit to being baffled by them. It seems effortless for you to get along with them."

"Training, practice and a genuine liking for them makes it easy," Melissa said, wondering how far she could go in expounding the need for more involvement with Alaya, Hamid and Nadia. "The best time to bond would be now when they are so lost from the death of their parents. And I do understand other commitments. Most of the parents for whom I watch their children are very busy. But the entire reason for having children is for family, don't you think?"

"These children are not mine."

"They are your family. You are talking about getting married and having a family, so this is your practice run." Melissa almost held her breath at her boldness. Would he get angry?

"I had a tutor when I was young, before I went to school in England," Surim said slowly.

"But you must have family memories. Special days spent with your mother and father. Holidays spent together. Birthdays."

He shook his head. "My father was too busy dealing with the various factions in the country. It was a difficult time in our history. My mother was sickly and didn't spend much time with me. They died together, returning from a visit to the Red Sea."

"You spent time with Mara. That was family." Maybe the man had no idea of how a proper family was to behave. The thought astonished her. Yet, if he'd had a lonely childhood, not been around children since, he probably didn't have a clue. For a moment, she felt sorry for the powerful man seated near her. Her own childhood had been happy and she had wonderful memories of the many things she and her mother had done together. How deplorable of his family to not insure every child had similar memories.

"Indeed. And in her memory, I am doing what I can for her children."

Melissa put her saucer back on the tray and rose. "Thank you for sharing the tea. I'm going to bed now."

He rose instantly. "I'll walk up with you. It is growing late and I have an early appointment in the morning."

They walked up the stairs and Surim escorted her to her bedroom door.

"Good night," she said.

"I regret I cannot fulfill your expectations as guardian for these children," he said.

"Of course you can. If you wish to."

"You believe that?"

"Absolutely. In no time, you'll wonder how you ever had a life before kids." She grinned at him.

"Sounds like a double-edged sword," he said, studying her expression.

Melissa laughed. "It can be. Let us know which evening we can all have dinner together. And any time you can spare to spend with them will help."

He leaned a bit closer and Melissa caught her breath. Was he going to kiss her?

"Good night, Melissa," Surim said and covered her lips with his.

For a split second she didn't move, then she stepped closer, reveling in the touch of his mouth against hers. When his arms enveloped her she slid her own around his powerful form, clinging as the embrace filled her with sensual delight. She had never felt so feminine and powerful as when kissing Surim.

His tongue brushed against her lips and she opened to him, letting him deepen the kiss. Conscious thought fled, right and wrong and danger disappeared. There was only this moment and this man.

A moment later he was gone, walking down the hall without a backward look.

Melissa stared after him long after he entered his bedroom and closed the door.

CHAPTER SIX

THE next afternoon Melissa sat down with the construction company's papers while Alaya read her book and Hamid and Nadia napped. The changes were minor, but she knew Max would want to be kept current on everything. It didn't take long to complete the translations. When she was finished, she headed downstairs to find someone to send them back to Surim's office for facsimile transmission to England. She felt better about leaving Max, knowing she was able to continue helping from Qu'Arim.

When the children were awake, she took them to the garden to play. She loved the beach, but wanted to make sure they had a variety of activities.

They had just finished dinner when the servant Melissa was getting used to seeing appeared in the nursery. He spoke rapidly to Annis, then turned to Melissa and spoke in French. "There is a telephone call for you. Please come with me."

"I'll be right back," she told the children and rose.

He led her to the study where a phone receiver was lying on the desk. Melissa picked it up, wondering if Max had a question on her translations.

"This is Melissa," she said.

"Hi, honey, how are you?" It was her mother.

"Mum, why are you calling? Is everything all right?"

"Fine here, dear. But I have some bad news for you. The

McDonalds called here a few minutes ago to cancel your contract. They're sending you extra money as a severance fee and hope you'll understand. Apparently their current nanny's plans for marriage fell through and she wants to remain with the children. And this after you gave up your job in Switzerland. What will you do?"

Melissa sat down in the chair. She'd been counting on that job.

Surim's words echoed in her mind—he'd offered her a position of some sort. She wasn't clear on what he expected.

She no longer had the Boston assignment; she could take one with him—if she dared. She couldn't imagine working with Surim, getting closer to him as they integrated the children into his household. Especially when he married and brought a suitable wife into the mix.

Maybe she could stay for just a little longer. She was already quite fond of the children. It would be easier for them to make the transition to the family with a familiar face. She spoke their language, though they had all started Arabic lessons this week.

"I might have the chance to remain here," she said slowly. This was something that would definitely take some thinking about. Right now she was a guest; if she went to work for Surim, her status would change instantly.

"A job? Or to continue the visit?"

"A job. I'll have to consider it. So I won't be home soon."

"Max and Robert were talking last night at dinner about the new restaurant in Qu'Arim. We're planning to fly out for the opening. I would love that. Do you think you'd work for the restaurant?"

"I'm not sure. But I do plan to come see the resort when it's completed. The setting is beautiful, and I expect the entire resort will be first class plus. Max is making sure the restaurant is perfect and it can only enhance their reputation," said Melissa. "Anyway, that's enough about the restaurant. How are things going?"

She and her mother chatted for another few minutes before

hanging up. She sat in the chair feeling torn. She had liked the McDonalds and their children. Had looked forward to caring for an infant as well.

If only she could segregate her feelings for her new boss, she might just have the chance of a place here.

The next few days went by without Melissa or the children seeing Surim. Annis related that he had asked after the children one night after they had gone to bed.

Fortunately for the household, Hamid's nightmares seemed a thing of the past. The little boy played hard all day, then slept soundly. Alaya was blossoming and wasn't sad as often as she'd been at first. Melissa hoped they were starting to feel as if they belonged.

Between Melissa and Annis, the children were prompted for good manners and encouraged in proper etiquette at each meal. Annis was also teaching them all basic words in Arabic. Sometimes they tried to hold a conversation, but no one knew enough words to make complete sentences. Hamid learned quickly. Nadia didn't even try. Alaya complained, but her accent was the best.

After breakfast on Thursday, Melissa received a summons to the study.

She entered a few moments later. Surim glanced up from a paper he was reading. "That was fast." He rose and indicated a chair.

"We just finished breakfast. You could have joined us."

"I shall make a note of that. This afternoon I plan to take the children to see Tante Tazil, their grandmother. I wish you to accompany us."

"That would be great. I know they would love to see her." She hadn't seen him since his kiss the other evening. She longed to ask what he'd been doing. Or even why he'd kissed her. Involuntarily, her gaze was drawn to his lips.

"That remains to be seen. She is quite depressed. I do hope seeing them will cheer her up, not bring unhappy memories. I heard their laughter the other evening. They are changing."

"You need to—"

"Spend more time with them," he finished for her. "I know. I am arranging my schedule to accommodate that. But some things can't be changed. Are you settling in all right?"

"Yes, thank you."

He leaned back in his chair and steepled his fingers. "I hear you had a phone call the other afternoon."

"Yes, from my mother."

"She is well, I trust."

Melissa smiled. "Of course. And looking forward to the opening of the Bella Lucia here in Qu'Arim. Robert has promised they will attend the event."

"I look forward to meeting her. Was there anything else?"

"Like?" she asked warily. He knew her job had been canceled; she'd bet a bundle on it.

"Like have you given more thought to my offer of a permanent job here?"

"In light of my other one being canceled, do you mean?" she asked. Max, he had to have told Surim.

"I heard that. I am surprised you didn't tell me sooner."

"I'm still debating if I wish to take advantage of your offer."

"I would raise the salary higher."

"I don't need it higher than the going rate," she said. Was that the way all businessmen thought? Throw more money at a situation to solve a problem?

"Shall we discuss concessions again?" he asked.

She looked at him sharply. Was he teasing? His face looked grave, but she suspected a lurking amusement in his eyes.

"Such as?"

"I have no idea. You had a list when I asked you to stay initially."

"And you are not fulfilling your part. What part of spending time with those children do you not get? A few hours one afternoon isn't enough to last all week."

"Dinner tonight."

"What?"

"We'll all have dinner tonight." She saw a glint of amusement in his eyes. "That will add to my score card."

Melissa frowned. "This isn't a game."

His dark eyes lost their amused expression. "No, I realize that. Shall we leave around one?"

"You realize Nadia usually naps at that time. Forgoing that could make her cranky."

"Ah. What would be a better time?"

"Three."

"Then I'll see you at three."

Melissa rose and headed for the door.

"And I hope to have your answer at that time, as well," he said.

She paused. "Exactly what would be my duties?" she asked.

He looked thoughtful for a moment. "About what they are now?"

"Hardly worth paying me for," she replied. "I think I had better return home soon. But I'll stay a little longer."

"The offer stands," he said, once again picking up the paper and scanning the report.

Surim didn't look up as Melissa left. He had been surprised when Max had mentioned on the phone yesterday that Melissa's job in the United States had been canceled. She had said nothing to him. Did she not wish to continue being with the children? Now that she was settling in, he could see the difference she made. Annis still gave a lot of the daily care, and he would not let her go. But the children blossomed with Melissa.

And he found her conversation refreshing. He placed the paper on the desk and leaned back, remembering her list of demands when he had first enlisted her help. He could just imagine an additional list if she stayed full-time.

What would it be like to have her give him a report each day on how the children progressed? She'd have her own unique slant on things. She reminded him of some of the girls he'd known when he'd lived in the UK. Bold, outspoken, confident in their own self-worth. Most of the younger women of his country were shy and quiet and never voiced an opinion until they knew what was expected. Then it mostly mirrored his own.

Not that he wanted anyone to argue with him, but sometimes it was refreshing that she had no agenda. She said what she thought. Would that change if she became dependent on him for her livelihood? He hoped not.

For a moment he thought about the other evening. He'd have to hold onto his emotions and not give way to impulse as he had with that kiss. It would be totally unsuitable in an employer-employee relationship.

He needed her. He hadn't a clue how to relate to those children. The three weeks in his care prior to Melissa's arrival proved that.

His thoughts turned to his need for a wife. Would he find a suitable bride soon? If so, within a year he could have his own son or daughter to raise. It was hard to picture, but he knew for the stability of his small country he needed to proceed and with haste. He was already in his late thirties. He hoped to live a long life, and not die before his son was an adult and trained to take over the reins of government.

For a moment Surim remembered his resentment and anger when his father had died. He had still been in school, had planned to study medicine. His father's brother could have assumed the leadership position, had he not been killed in one of the armed skirmishes two months prior to Surim's father's death.

Instead, Surim had been summoned home and plunged into politics with a vengeance. For years he'd had private tutors to educate him to college levels; all the while he'd been learning how to rule a fractious country. His ministers had helped, good strong men his father had chosen.

Surim gazed out the window, lost in thought. Some days he still wished he had become a doctor. There was a great need for medically trained people in the world, and he wanted to make a difference.

He had, but in a totally different manner than he'd dreamed of as a boy.

Ah, well, the dreams of childhood were not necessarily meant to be fulfilled. He turned back to the endless paperwork and began to review an updated report from the construction firm building the resort. This project was important. Not only to forge new ties with European countries, but to bring another source of cash to their economy. He didn't want Qu'Arim to be a one-industry nation. He had until three o'clock to get through some of the work that waited. Then he could take time with Melissa without guilt. He looked forward to it.

Melissa made sure the children were ready prior to three. It was a bit tight with Nadia waking only a few moments before the hour. Still, all were washed, brushed and in clean clothes at the appointed hour.

They went down the stairs, Hamid chattering a mile a minute. Such a difference from when she'd first arrived.

Melissa wore one of the suits she'd brought for her business dealings. She hoped the boxes of clothes her mother had sent would arrive soon.

The four of them arrived in the foyer just as Surim came from his office. He looked wonderful in his dark suit and pristine white shirt. Melissa had to force her attention back to Alaya as she jumped up and down with excitement. She'd much rather just eat Surim up with her eyes!

"Are we really going to see Grandmama? I haven't seen her

since the funeral; she was wearing all black and crying. I was crying, too, because I wanted my mummy and daddy. But now we're here. It will be fun, won't it?" she asked anxiously.

"She misses your mother, as you all do," Melissa said gently, brushing back the hair flying around with the child's jumping and feeling a little surprised Alaya had attended the funeral. "She'll be happy to see you. And you'll have happier memories after today. I know seeing her upset at the funeral must have upset you. Children need adults to be strong. But your mum was her only daughter and she was sad. Today she'll be happier for seeing you and your brother and sister." Melissa remembered Surim had mentioned the woman was suffering deep depression at the loss of her only child. She hoped the children's visit brought her spirits up.

"She's not going to die, is she?" Hamid asked.

Surim paused and looked at Melissa.

"Not any time soon. So tell me what you plan to say to your grandmother," Melissa said.

The three children recited, 'Hello, Grandmother,' in Arabic.

"Well done," Surim said. He looked at Melissa. "And you?"

"I'm happy to make your acquaintance," she said in perfect Arabic.

"I'm impressed."

"Annis is teaching us," Melissa said, pleased at his compliment.

The drive was short, lasting less than ten minutes. The house was impressive, with ornate plaster around the windows and handsomely carved doors.

Surim had called and talked with Tante Tazil that morning. She had still sounded as if the act of talking were more than she could do, but had said she'd be happy to see the children. He hoped the visit helped all of them, and didn't cause any problems with the children.

They were ushered into a sunroom. The sky was cloudless

and the room was filled with sunshine, flowering plants and light furnishings.

Melissa held Nadia's hand, and the other two children crowded around her, warily watching the older woman as they approached where she sat in one of the chairs.

She seemed older than Melissa had expected. Yet maybe the death of her daughter had aged her.

Surim beckoned them closer, clearly introducing Melissa. She spoke her phrase in Arabic and the older woman looked surprised. She replied rapidly and Melissa was totally lost.

Surim said something and the woman nodded, switching to French. "I thank you for taking care of my grandchildren. I am unable to manage at this time."

"They are delightful." Melissa urged them closer and murmured in their ears.

"Hello, Grandmother," they chorused.

She held out her arms and they ran to hug her. Tears spilled from her eyes. "My precious ones," she whispered in English. "I am happy to see you all."

In only a few moments she sat back, dabbed at her eyes, and smiled at the children. "I will have cakes and biscuits brought up."

She looked at Melissa. "If you like, I will ask for tea. I know the English like tea."

"Actually, Tante, I thought to show Melissa your gardens while you and the children visit," Surim said. "Melissa enjoys flowers, and your garden is beautiful."

"Grown a bit wild lately, I think," she said sadly, then gazed at the children. "But a good idea. You can report back on the work needed. Come, children, tell me all you've been doing since you arrived."

Surim led Melissa to the garden. It was quite tiny in comparison to his. Obviously a bit out of hand, as well.

"Tante Tazil is her own gardener, and I think has neglected things in her sadness," he said. "Do you recognize the flowers?"

"Yes, I think I see old favorites everywhere," Melissa said.

"Are you an avid gardener?"

"No, my mother likes to work with dirt, but not me. Though I do love flowers, as you said. This is a pretty setting, but I like your garden better."

"What do you like to do in your free time?" Surim asked.

She looked at him, wondering if he ever had any free time. "I loved to ski in the winter in Switzerland. I like reading and exploring. I read about a place, then visit and explore as much as I can. The advantage of living in Switzerland was being so centralized in Europe. I had planned to do the same thing from Boston."

"Until your plans were changed."

She nodded.

"So you like it here?"

"Of course. But that doesn't mean I want to work for you," she said without thought.

"Oh?"

She glanced at him uneasily. "I like visiting," she said. Let him make what he would out of that.

They joined the others in the sunroom a short time later. Melissa thought the children's grandmother looked much happier than she had when they had arrived.

"You must leave so soon?"

"We've been here long enough," Surim said. "We will return again next week if you like. And you are always welcome to visit at my house; you know that."

"Maybe I shall." Tante Tazil turned her attention to Melissa. "Would you mind taking the children into the garden for a moment? I wish to speak to His Excellency alone."

Surim watched as Melissa nodded and herded the children outside. He could guess what the older woman wished to talk about.

"I understand you are looking for a wife, Surim," she said, confirming his suspicions.

Surim nodded warily. "Even sequestered as you, Tante, you seem to know what is going on."

"You can't keep a secret; did you think you could? It is on the mind of everyone—whom shall you choose? I know a young woman who would be suitable. She was friends with Mara when they were young."

Surim involuntarily glanced through the window at Melissa. She was talking with Alaya and holding Nadia. For a moment, he could envision her holding a child of his. How would such an unsuitable match be perceived by his country?

"Surim?" Tante Tazil said sharply. She followed his gaze and frowned. "I do hope the children won't become too attached to the Englishwoman. The woman I'm thinking about has studied in Paris, so has a worldly cosmopolitan outlook that should appeal to you. Yasine bin Shora. I shall invite you both to dinner this week."

"I shall look forward to meeting her," Surim said. For a moment he considered telling his aunt he had prior engagements at dinner—eating with the children. But he didn't think she'd approve.

Surim called Melissa back in, and Tazil smiled at each of the children as they hugged her goodbye.

"Next week if I'm feeling better, you can come again."

"Do feel free to come visit at my house any time you wish, Tante Tazil," Surim said, giving her a kiss on her cheek. "Just let Melissa know so she can make sure the children are there."

"The sooner you find a wife, the better. You should not have waited so long," his aunt chided him.

Surim felt the restrictions of his position close in on him. Usually he didn't mind the challenges of leadership. But the pressure from his ministers, and now family, were daunting. He understood the need for an heir to insure a smooth transition of power when he died. But he didn't like the constant pressure to find a woman right away.

As he settled in the limousine he watched Melissa. She was a beautiful woman. Good things came in small packages—wasn't that an old English saying? Her eyes sparkled as she listened to Hamid. Nadia remained close, seeming a bit listless. Alaya sat next to him.

"Did you have a good time?" he asked.

"She's very old, isn't she?" Alaya said.

"No. But she is very sad because of your mother's death. Being around you and the others will help her get her energy back and then you won't think she's so old."

"I wish Melissa would stay forever. Can't you make her?"

Surim shook his head. "I can't force her to remain. But I will do my best to see if she can stay with us until you and the others are all grown up."

"I should like that!"

So would I, Surim thought, a bit startled at the knowledge. He looked at Melissa again, wanting her to smile at him as she did so easily for Hamid.

When they reached the house, Surim asked Melissa to remain while the children ran up to the nursery.

"Dinner will not be private and I wish to discuss your remaining here for the foreseeable future," he said. He led the way to the living room, shutting the doors behind them. "Do sit down," he invited, waiting for her to sit on the sofa before joining her. The fragrance of her perfume filled the air. Light and sweet. Not a bit cloying like Delleah's was sometimes.

"I can't stay beyond a few weeks," she said.

"So tell me the stumbling points and I'll see what I can address."

She remained silent, thinking. Her eyes roamed around the room, settling nowhere, and not looking at him.

"You like the children," he said to break the silence.

"Yes."

"Is it me you have a problem with?"

She shook her head. Then hesitated. "No, no problem I can't deal with."

Ah, there was something. His curiosity rose. "And that would be?"

"Nothing I can't deal with. I guess I just need time to think about staying. You're getting married; don't you think your future wife should have some say in who watches the children? Especially when you have your own children. She may not wish me to be part of your household."

"That won't be any time soon. If you prefer, we can arrange a six-month period."

"What if I don't suit?" she asked.

"I can't imagine that. But either party has the right to terminate before six months. And either way, I'll give you a severance package equal to six months' pay, to give you time to find another position that suits you."

"That's more generous than I need," she protested.

"But what I propose."

"Let me think about it." She rose and headed for the stairs, pausing at the doorway to look back at him. "I appreciate the offer. I'm just not sure I can do it." And she was absolutely certain she couldn't tell him the reason.

As Melissa went upstairs she admitted her attraction to Surim was growing stronger daily. She had no business even holding out hope she'd remain. Her best plan would be to stay another week, then get back to England where she'd be safe.

Maybe if she could focus on the children and virtually ignore Surim, she'd have a chance. Just because he set her heart racing every time she saw him was no reason to let him occupy her every waking moment.

He was seeking a wife. Melissa hoped he would find someone special. He deserved a wife who loved him, who wanted to make his life easier, and share the ups and downs. She wished he'd look her way. Not that she stood a chance. She wasn't even from Qu'Arim, and she could just imagine what people would think of their leader marrying a foreigner. For a split second, however, she remembered another leader who had given up a throne for the woman he loved. Love was the difference.

Melissa took a few moments to freshen up, then headed for the nursery. Tonight was dinner with Surim in the main dining room. Only Alaya and Hamid were participating. Nadia was too young. Annis would see she got her dinner as usual.

"Ready?" she asked when she arrived.

"Do we have to?" Alaya asked. "Uncle Surim will want us to have perfect manners and I want to eat and then play."

"Me, too," Hamid piped up.

"We can play another evening. Tonight we are dining with your uncle."

The long table in the dining room had been set. Melissa was pleased to note everyone was clustered near the head, rather than spaced out. It wasn't going to be a cozy dinner, but at least she would be near the children and Surim. No shouting needed.

"Remember all I taught you?" Melissa asked as she and the children went to the seats on either side of the table.

"Yes, sit quietly. Speak when spoken to," Alaya said.

"Use our napkins!" Hamid shouted, then laughed.

Melissa relaxed. She hoped the meal would be enjoyable and not stressful. She planned to do her best to make it so.

The conversation centered on the afternoon's visit to the children's grandmother. Melissa was pleased with the way Alaya and Hamid were behaving.

The entire meal went much better than breakfast a few days earlier had gone. Still, Melissa was tired from the stress by the time the children were excused. She rose to take them upstairs, but Surim shook his head.

"They know the way; they've explored the house on many occasions. Annis will put them to bed. Stay."

Alaya gave Melissa a hug and then Hamid, not to be outdone, came round the table to give her a hug.

"Will you read me a story before I go to sleep?" he asked.

"I'll be up in a little while. If you fall asleep before I get there, I'll read you two tomorrow, how's that?" Melissa asked, tousling the boy's hair. She was coming to love these precious children.

"I want a story, too," Alaya said, leaning against Melissa.

"Same deal. Now bid your uncle good night and scoot upstairs."

Hamid approached Surim slowly. When Surim pushed back his chair and beckoned, Hamid went to give him a hug. Alaya followed.

"Good night," they called and raced from the room.

Surim looked at Melissa. "Pass or fail?" he asked.

She laughed. "This wasn't a test. It was a family dinner. And I think it went well, but what I think doesn't matter as much as what you think."

"Surprisingly, I enjoyed it," he said.

"Why the surprise? They're super children."

"It is not the custom in my family to have children at the meals until they are almost adults."

"Who made that rule?" Melissa asked before she thought. "Oops, of course your customs are important, but it is nice to have the children share in family activities. How do you grow close if you don't?"

"Shall we have coffee in the salon? These chairs are not made for endless hours." Surim rose and escorted Melissa to the informal salon. The French doors were opened to the gardens. Faint illumination came from the lighting outside. The lamps had been lit in the salon.

She sat on the sofa and watched as he paced to the doors and paused.

"One reason my father sent me to school in England was to expand my knowledge of other societies. He had gone to school in France. His brother in Italy. So it was England's turn."

Melissa watched him. Where was this leading?

Surim turned and looked at her. "But boarding school is different from family life. I went home a few times with Max, who enjoyed a very different family life from my own."

Melissa's own family had been comprised of only her mother and herself after her father's death. They'd done many things together, from sharing meals and shopping trips to planning holidays together. All memories Melissa would cherish forever.

"The upshot is I'm not familiar with the English way of doing things."

"And you're not sure you want that for the children?"

"Actually, I think it might be a good way to make them initially feel safe and secure. I know Mara and Anwar spent a lot of time with the children. They loved living in England."

But you aren't sure how to go on, Melissa surmised. "So you do what English families do: have meals together, spend time in the evenings doing things as a family. Which usually means activities that can include the youngest child. Don't relegate them solely to the nursery."

Surim looked around the salon. "I will have the room made childproof."

"Or at least put the most valuable items away for a while. Children need to learn boundaries."

"I want them to feel free to roam everywhere. I didn't have that freedom when I was younger. I remember coming home at seventeen, suddenly in charge of the house. There were actually rooms I had never been inside."

Melissa was astonished. More so that he was revealing such personal items to her. What put him in such a revealing mood?

"Excellency, there is a phone call for you." One of the servants stood at the doorway, holding a portable phone.

"I'm busy," Surim said shortly.

"I wouldn't intrude except it is Madame ibn Horock and you are usually available for her."

"Tante Tazil," Surim said and crossed the room. "Excuse me a moment, Melissa; I do take her calls."

Melissa didn't know whether to leave or remain, but when he took the phone and stepped into the foyer she remained where she was. In only moments another man entered carrying a large tray with fragrant coffee and some small cakes. He placed the tray on the coffee table and said something to her in Arabic.

"Do you speak French?" she asked.

He replied in that language and indicated he would bring anything else needed.

"This looks perfect, thank you," she said and leaned forward to pour the coffee into the delicate cups. They were lovely, and seemed too delicate for Surim's strong hands.

Surim strode back into the room a few moments later. He sat on the chair near the sofa and Melissa handed him a cup of coffee.

"You take it black," she said.

"You noticed?"

"At your aunt's. Is she all right? Seeing the children wasn't too much for her, was it?" she asked.

"She is fine. In fact, she feels she's getting back to normal. That call was to arrange a dinner for me to meet a friend of Mara's Tante Tazil is convinced would make the perfect wife."

"How nice," Melissa said, taking a sip of her coffee and not looking at the man. She wished he had not taken the call, or at least not shared it with her. What would it be like to marry Surim? To live forever in this lovely home by the Persian Gulf?

The thoughts brought a flood of heat to her cheeks and she firmly pushed the idea away. There was no possibility he'd look at her.

Besides, if there wasn't a strong love bond in a marriage, she didn't want it. She'd thought she'd loved Paul, but now that she had had time to look back she realized she'd been in love with the idea of being in love. Paul had been dynamic and exciting and for a few brief months she'd felt like Cinderella at the ball. But there had been no lasting ties forged. Paul was about good times and fast living. She liked that, but she also liked evenings at home, doing little but relaxing. Paul had found those stifling.

She also put a high regard on fidelity, which Paul discounted as old-fashioned and out of vogue. Would he have felt the same if she'd been the one cheating? Probably, because he really hadn't loved her. He hadn't cared enough.

"You're very quiet," Surim said.

She looked up into his dark eyes, her heart catching. "I was just thinking about marriage, and how differently we view it."

"The western view is based on love," he said. "Yet your divorce rate is high, and, from what I saw when I lived there, not every union has an abundance of love."

"You're right. But for those who do, it's a special tie. My mother and father loved each other. She was a widow for twenty years before marrying Max's father last spring. She adores him and he her. I'm glad she didn't settle."

"Do you see an arranged marriage as settling?" Surim asked.

"No, I think that's even worse. What if you two don't suit? Will you have enough time in the courtship to get to know someone? Know whether or not you'll tolerate each other enough to live together for fifty or more years?" Melissa suddenly realized what she was saying—and to whom.

"Not that it's any of my business," she quickly added.

He smiled at her. "The interesting thing about you, Melissa, is that you don't treat me any differently than I imagine you treat your friends at home."

"We're hardly friends," she said, feeling uncomfortable.

"Maybe we could be," he suggested.

"I'm here for the children." And any overture of friendship would only go to making her fantasies more real. She needed to nip that attraction in the bud. If she wanted to succeed, she needed to remember the wide gulf between his position and hers. She had even less in common with him than she had with Paul.

But as she'd realized earlier, her growing feelings for Surim were stronger than anything she'd ever felt before. And where did that leave her?

CHAPTER SEVEN

OVER the next week Melissa and the children settled into a comfortable routine. They did Arabic lessons in the morning with Annis, and some catch-up lessons in English. They played outside in the afternoons. Twice it rained, so they spent time exploring the large house that was their new home.

Each evening, if Surim was home, he had them join him in the dining room for dinner—even little Nadia.

Melissa was pleased with the way the family was growing. Surim wasn't always home, and she tried not to worry about whom he was meeting and how the great marriage stakes were progressing.

The evenings he was home, he insisted she spend time with him in the salon after the children went to bed—ostensibly to review what they had done during the day. But while the conversation started with the children each night, it soon ranged to current events, to books they'd both read and talk of the new resort.

Melissa was emboldened to speak her mind when talking with Surim, as he seemed to like what she had to say, even when he didn't agree with her. Some evenings there were lively discussions when they opposed each other on a particular topic.

Always feeling revived and refreshed after spending an evening with Surim, Melissa wondered how he was faring in finding a wife. She hated the nights he was away, worried each morning he'd greet the children with news of his engagement.

He had not kissed her again. She knew she should be grateful not to get her emotions clouded over by the physical attraction she felt. Yet she wished he'd touch her, kiss her, hold her again. She'd never felt like that before, and was afraid no other man would make her feel exactly like that.

Yet she was being selfish. The children would benefit by having a new mother. It would make their family stronger, just as Surim had said. But until he announced an engagement, it would hurt no one if he stole a kiss or two.

Tonight he'd eaten with the children, but instead of leaving after the meal he sat in one of the large chairs brought up to the nursery.

"I thought tomorrow we would go shopping," he said.

"Shopping?" Melissa sat in the chair opposite his, cuddling Nadia in her lap. The child was looking at a picture book, pretending to be reading.

"Hamid, for one, needs some new clothes. And a haircut wouldn't go amiss either," Surim said. "I have arranged my schedule to have several hours free in the late morning. That way Nadia will be home in time for her nap."

He never forgot anything, she mused. And he was trying. The children seemed to be much more relaxed around him, but Surim himself needed to unbend a little more for her satisfaction. He didn't romp with them, or get silly. Was he too lost in protocol to bother?

"That would be wonderful. Would we shop the souks?" she asked.

Surim frowned, then shrugged. "If that's what you wish. I thought one of the stores on Amir Street, but we can see what the souks have."

"It'll be a good chance to practice our Arabic," she said.

"Indeed," agreed Surim. "How is your Arabic progressing?"

"Slowly coming," she replied in that tongue. "I do not have tenses in verbs. I can talk simple sentences. I can ask for food, the directions to the police station and a bathroom." She laughed, switching back to English. "I have a long way to go if I want to become fluent."

"And the children?"

"Hamid is fastest; he and Annis actually converse for several minutes. Alaya is getting the hang of it. Nadia can make simple sentences, but loses interest quickly. Once we know more, we can spend time each day speaking Arabic, which will help her adjust. It's a bit confusing, but there are bilingual children the world over. It's really easier to learn young."

"Tomorrow you can try your skills at the souks."

Melissa smiled. "That'll for sure brand me a tourist, then they'll raise the prices."

Surim was always amused by Melissa's practice of economy. Had she no idea how much money he had at his disposal? The children in their own rights had enough income to live comfortably even if they never worked. But she looked for bargains, and seemed more conservative of his spending than he.

"I believe I can talk them down to a reasonable level," he said.

"They won't recognize you, will they?" she asked.

"I have no idea. I haven't visited the souks since I was a teenager."

She gave it some thought. He'd love to know what she was worried about now.

"Maybe the children and I should go alone," she said a moment later.

"I assure you I can manage at the souks."

"But won't the crowds be dangerous or something?"

"I doubt most of the people will recognize me, or expect me to be shopping for rock-bottom prices."

She smiled at that, and Surim was again struck by how

lovely she was. Her green eyes fascinated him. Sometimes they were as clear as glass, other times they reminded him of mossy stream beds, deep and mysterious.

Alaya came and climbed into his lap, snuggling up against him. For a moment Surim savored the feeling her trust gave him. She was warming up the fastest, because of his stories of their mother.

"Tell me another story about Mummy," she said.

"How about when she was eight years old and fell down the stairs?" he began, recounting the story with some embellishments to make Mara look heroic. He and his cousin had been close growing up—at least during the summer months when he'd been home from boarding school. His love for England had filled her head and when she'd had the chance to move there, she'd jumped at it. She'd loved the freedom and excitement of London and had often talked to him over the last few years about her experiences.

She had raised her children more British than Qu'Arimian. He didn't begrudge her her happiness, especially in light of her early death.

He watched Melissa as he talked about his cousin. What kind of mother would she make? From what he'd observed over the last few days, she'd be very involved with her children.

At least she wouldn't be a doormat or yes-woman as the last couple of women he'd been seeing had proved. Yasine, the woman his Tante Tazil had introduced to him, had seemed the perfect match at the beginning. She was beautiful with dark eyes and long dark hair. Her manners were perfect. Her ability to make conversation on any topic would stand her in good stead in official functions.

But she didn't appear to have a thought of her own. Either she parroted what her father said, or waited for Surim to express his opinion and then concurred. Nice to a degree, but he found he liked a more stimulating discourse. And talking with Melissa was guaranteed to give him that.

In fact, he was in danger of letting his pursuit of a wife

dwindle, looking forward more to spending the evenings with the children and their guest.

One of his aides had commented on the fact that time was passing and had asked if he'd found a suitable bride. The ministers wanted the succession assured. It was not fair to the country to leave it in chaos if he should die suddenly.

Yet he hesitated. Maybe he'd absorbed more of western philosophy than he'd expected. He was not looking for love in a mate, but he did want someone compatible. Someone he could see himself spending fifty years with.

Melissa had planted that thought and now he couldn't shake it.

She looked up then and smiled at the picture of Alaya sitting on his lap. The little girl was thrilled to learn more about her mother. Even Hamid had left the train set he was building to sit near Surim's chair, enraptured with the tale. Who would have thought twenty-some years later Mara's breaking her ankle would make such an enthralling tale?

"You're good at that," Melissa said when he finished.

"Telling about the past?"

"And making it fascinating. Did Mara really do all those things?"

"She was an amazing young girl. So, now, off to bed. I see Annis at the doorway," Surim said, rising. He gave each child a hug, wishing again his cousin had lived.

"If you have time, perhaps you would join me in the study," he said to Melissa.

They needed to discuss plans for the next day. And he had another question to ask. One that would likely surprise her.

She joined him a short time later, having read the children a short story.

"Tomorrow, I have to leave early. The limo will come for you at ten, swing by and pick me up and we'll head to the souks. Practice your Arabic."

"Great, but please don't throw me to the wolves. They'll see I'm British from a mile away so you'll need to do the bargaining. I think the children will be thrilled."

"The children or you?"

She laughed. "Okay, I confess, I've been dying to go since I arrived. How perfect to have a translator with me."

"My services don't come cheap," he said, finding the perfect lead into what he wanted to ask.

"Oh?" Her merry smile brought one from him.

"I have an invitation to a reception at the British Consulate Saturday. I thought you might like to attend with me."

Melissa's eyes widened in surprise. "Well, if that's OK… Yes, I should love to. What time?"

"It begins at eight. Apparently the Consulate General is being replaced and his successor will be presented. He has already called on my office and I think he's brighter than the one leaving. You'll enjoy meeting him."

"Wait," she said suddenly. "Shouldn't you be taking one of your prospects?"

"Prospects?"

"Prospective wife. Over the last week, your evenings have been spent more and more with the children, leaving little courting time. Maybe you should ask someone else."

"I ask whom I wish and for this event it is you." How dared she second-guess him? Or tell him who to invite? She was as bad as his aides.

"Yes, Your Excellency." She gave a mock curtsey, which should have annoyed him, but almost made him laugh. "So what shall I say to the new Consulate?"

"Easy. You can tell him how much you love living here and never wish to leave."

She paused for a moment. Surim wondered what he had said to cause that odd look on her face. Then she smiled. "That's fair enough. Especially after I have a chance to go shopping and see more of Qu'Arim. You realize I've been here several weeks and have only raced through town, and seen the resort site a few times?"

"How remiss. I shall take a day or two off and take you to the desert, as we once spoke of in the gardens. How would you like that?"

"I should love it. When?"

"After the reception. We'll leave the children with Annis and fly to somewhere special."

"Your secret oasis?"

He nodded.

Melissa smiled brightly. "I'd be thrilled."

Surim wasn't sure he was doing the wise thing. Once she was there, he'd forever picture her when he visited. Still, he'd like to share that part of himself with her. He had a feeling Melissa would truly love it, just as she'd said.

He wanted Melissa to like Qu'Arim. To stay to keep the children happy.

"Saturday I thought we'd explore one of the pearl farms, and then attend the reception. The children shall spend the day with Annis."

"Oh, but—"

"No buts; it is decided."

Surim needed to work on his autocratic manner, Melissa thought wryly, then looked at him. He was the leader of an important country. He'd had the role thrust on him when he should have still been enjoying being a teenager. If he was a bit overbearing, it was excusable. But if she was staying for long, they would surely clash more than once.

"Tomorrow the limo will arrive at ten," Surim repeated in dismissal.

"Thank you, that would be lovely." Melissa rose and headed for the door. "I'll see you then."

He looked at her with his dark eyes and her heart flipped over. Did he have any idea what he could do to a woman's equilibrium? She bid him good night and hurried off to her bedroom. Saturday he wanted to spend the day with her. And the evening. Without the children. She could hardly wait.

Reaching her room, she closed the door and did a little dance of excitement. She was going to see a pearl farm, and be escorted to a Consulate reception by the world's sexiest man. And then see his desert oasis. Just the two of them.

Would he kiss her?

Would she kiss him?

Stopping dead, she shook her head. That would only lead to disaster. He was doing all this merely as a courtesy to Max. A sheikh certainly didn't take out a nanny! Unless—for a moment she wondered if he was showing her all the advantages to living in Qu'Arim so she'd stay. Was it a bribe to get his way? Maybe she should give him her answer one way or the other and see what happened.

Surim drew a folder close, prepared to do a little work before retiring. Salid, one of his trusted aides, entered through the opened door, a sheaf of papers in hand.

"I have the reports on Yasine bin Shora and her family, Excellency. There is no subversive activity that we could find."

Surim held out his hand for the report. It was unfortunate that the ministry insisted on a background check for any woman he showed an interest in. He knew it was for the future good of the country, but it felt invasive and in bad taste.

He had not read the one for Delleah and her family; he would not read this one.

In fact, though he knew the importance of getting married, he was losing interest in the entire process.

He'd much rather spend time with Melissa. Wouldn't that interest the ministers?

"Thanks, Salid. Get to bed. I will not be working tomorrow. You may take the day off as well. Spend it with your family."

The aide looked surprised. "Thank you, sir. I shall."

Surim contemplated the outing tomorrow. It had been a long time since he'd taken a day off for pure foolish pleasure. Maybe he was working too hard, as Max had suggested.

His pet project was the new resort. He was constantly battling those who opposed it; those who wished to keep foreigners out. They didn't realize how much money would pour into the country with a lively tourist trade. Schools would be a primary benefit. And health care for the nomads who still roamed the desert. The proof would come, but until then it was an uphill fight.

He planned to discuss the possibility of tourists viewing the pearl farm Saturday, combining business with pleasure. Melissa would be a good source to learn what would appeal and what wouldn't.

Melissa awoke with anticipation. She'd wanted to visit the souks since she'd first learned she was coming to Qu'Arim. The exotic open-air markets had long fascinated her. She'd visited open-air markets in Spain and Germany, but couldn't wait to see what the local one had to offer.

She reviewed her clothes, wishing the box of things her mother had shipped would arrive. If it didn't get here soon, she might be leaving before it arrived. She had one sundress that she could wear without the jacket, making it a bit more informal. Other than that, she had little to wear. Maybe she'd find some clothes for herself as well as for the children.

For Saturday night, she wondered if she'd have time to find another dress and not have to wear the blue gown she'd worn to the reception Surim had given. She still had her dress from home, but would love something special.

But at the same time, she had to keep her feet on the ground.

She could not start daydreaming about being the woman of his choice. He'd said the reception was at the British Consulate and he'd invited her to mingle with some of her countrymen. He was being kind. She would not read anything more into it than that.

By the time Melissa arrived at the nursery, the children were halfway through their breakfast; Surim was nowhere to be seen.

Annis greeted her and for several stilted moments Melissa practiced her Arabic. The older woman never laughed, but her eyes twinkled quite a bit with Melissa's attempts.

"His Excellency told me to remind you he would be sending a car at ten to transport you and the children to the souks." Annis frowned. "It is crowded with unsavory persons there. Why would he take you to the souks?"

"I asked. I think it will be great fun."

"Is easier at the boutiques, I think."

Melissa smiled and shook her head. "This will be an adventure, for me and the children," she replied.

Promptly at ten she shepherded the children downstairs to the waiting limousine.

Hamid had a thousand questions about the vehicle. Ascertaining the driver spoke limited English, Melissa prevailed upon him to allow Hamid to ride in the front seat, securely belted, and answer all his questions.

She and the girls sat in regal splendor in the back.

"There's even a television," Alaya said, flicking on the unit. The program was in Arabic. She watched for a moment, then flicked it off. "I miss our telly. All of these are in Arabic."

"Oh, come on, Alaya, we have much better things to do than watch TV." Melissa smiled. "Do you remember your lessons in deportment at a souk?"

"Don't seem interested; don't touch anything. And always smile and say thank you if we buy something. It's the same as Mummy used to say."

"Good, you want to act as your mum wanted."

Alaya rummaged in the small purse she carried and fished out a photo. "This is the last picture I have. It's sort of small." She handed it to Melissa.

The young couple looked happy, smiling into the camera. Their dark good looks had been passed to their children. Melissa's heart ached at their deaths. How sad for all that the children would grow up without their parents.

She couldn't imagine growing up without her mother. Granted, now her life took her far away from the small flat they'd shared off Fleet Street, but she'd had the strong grounding of her mother's love as she'd grown, and they were only a phone call away these days.

With her mother's recent marriage, Melissa felt as if a big step had been taken away from her. Her mother loved her dearly, she knew that, but Melissa was no longer the sole light in her mother's world.

Melissa wondered if she'd ever find love, marry and raise a family. She loved working with children. Couldn't imagine not having kids of her own. But the man would have to be very special.

The limousine slid to a stop. The driver jumped out and ran around to open the passenger door with a flourish. Surim stepped into the vehicle.

Instantly Melissa felt as if the air had been compressed. Her heart fluttered again and she wanted to fling herself into his arms.

Shocked, she scooted as far from where he sat as she could. Had thinking about her mother's romance addled her brains? Surim Al-Thani was her host! Nothing more.

But he was a man. She threw a quick glance at him as he engaged Nadia and Alaya in conversation. A gorgeous man, with dark eyes and lashes so long she was envious. His suit was filled out perfectly. She had seen him at the beach, and now dressed for business. He'd looked fabulous in the tux when he'd held the reception in Max's honor. Did the man ever appear the slightest bit ragged?

He looked at her, capturing her gaze with his. She wanted to look away, but couldn't.

"Are you looking forward to shopping?" he asked.

"Very much so. Will there be pearls in some of the stalls?"

"Undoubtedly. But wait until we go to the pearl farm to purchase any. The prices will be lowest there."

The limousine stopped near the edge of the vast open-air market. They exited the car, and Melissa noticed a black sedan pulled in right behind them, two familiar men in suits climbing out.

"Your friends accompany us, I see," she said.

"They are here to make sure there are no incidents. The souks can get crowded and the children are small."

"Is there danger?" Melissa asked. She had never considered such a thing. Yet Surim was a very wealthy man. Even if he had few enemies, some unscrupulous crook could try to kidnap the children for ransom.

"Only from them getting lost. We pride ourselves on having one of the lowest crime rates in the world. Come, you are safe here."

CHAPTER EIGHT

THE souks were all Melissa had ever imagined. The open-air stalls seemed to go on forever. There were clear dividing lines between each one, with large banners hanging from the canopies, all with beautiful Arabic script, of course. She was just learning to speak the language; would she ever learn to read it?

As she walked down the crowded path she noticed several shops had placards proclaiming they spoke French or Italian or German or English. She could hear the chatter of a number of languages. Dress consisted of formal Arab robes, carefree tourist attire, and even conservative business suits.

There was a buzz of excitement in the air and everyone seemed to be enjoying the day. People bargained for prices, some quite demonstratively, others quietly. The shopkeepers seemed to enjoy the process as much as their customers.

Mounds of spices were first as they plunged into the crowded aisle, heaps of fragrant ginger, nutmeg, and other exotic seasonings. Then several booths of fresh fruit and, beyond, fish caught that morning.

"Is this like a food market? I thought there'd be clothes and things," she asked Surim after a moment.

"You can buy anything here. Come this way," Surim said as he wove his way through the throngs of people examining the merchandise. In another couple of minutes they were in a completely different area, with luxurious rugs displayed, olive wood and acacia carvings for sale. She saw bolts of fabric at one stall.

"This one will make up any item of clothing you wish; just pick out the material and let them take your measurements," he said, stopping to converse with the merchant.

Melissa kept tight hold of Nadia's hand. She made sure she had Alaya and Hamid in sight at all times. She didn't want to dampen the children's enthusiasm with too many restrictions. Still, this kind of shopping was quite different from what they were used to.

The variety of wares was amazing. From ornate furnishings to strands of gold necklaces. Pearls large and small; some set in fancy jewelry, some lying in shallow boxes for people to choose from. There was even a toy stall that had puzzles and sturdy wooden toys.

Nadia and Hamid loved that place best, spending long minutes trying out different ones.

"Shall I buy them each one toy?" Surim asked quietly in her ear. Melissa turned, bumping into him, he was so close. Yet where else would he go as the other shoppers crowded the wide aisles, jostling each other as they moved to close in on the best bargains? She stared at him, his face inches from her. For a moment the souks seemed to fade; there was just herself and Surim. She dragged her gaze away.

"It would be very nice, I think," she said. Surim leaned closer still to hear her and she could smell his aftershave. Its tangy scent started butterflies in her stomach, and she wished she could step away. Or step closer.

Drawing on her reserves, she smiled and eased back a few scant inches. "Nadia seems especially enchanted with that puzzle. I think it's perfect for a toddler. And Hamid likes the wooden trucks. He would be able to play with those at the beach as well." She hardly knew what she was saying. Every cell in her body seemed attuned to him.

"And Alaya—is she too old for toys?" he asked, the look in his eye suggesting he knew what she was thinking.

"No, but I think she was taken with some of the material at the place we passed a few moments ago. Maybe a sundress?"

"And you?"

"I'm having such fun. Haven't seen anything I must have, however. But I wouldn't mind a dress or two myself to tide me over until the clothes my mother is sending arrive. And there will be pearls to see on Saturday."

"A lovely strand to go to the reception that evening, perhaps?"

"I doubt I can afford a strand. But maybe a pair of earrings."

Surim said nothing, but narrowed his eyes slightly. Inclining his head once, he reached out to take her arm and pull her gently out of the way of some boisterous tourists.

"We'll buy the toys. One of the guards has located a stall with children's clothing. We will find what we need there."

The fascination held as they followed the guard and found several places to buy casual clothing for the children. Each was measured and an assortment of ready-made clothes was quickly held up for their choice. Selecting four outfits for each child, Melissa helped Nadia and Alaya, and kept an eye on Surim's assisting Hamid.

Just as they were ready to leave, Melissa spotted a lovely rich green silk. It would make a beautiful evening gown. And she wanted something grand for the embassy reception on Saturday.

"Wait a second, can you?" Not waiting for Surim's answer she turned to the shopkeeper and negotiated a price. Her measurements were taken and the fabric held up to the light. It shimmered with rich color, reflecting the sun.

"It will look beautiful on you," he said when she joined him a few moments later at the edge of the booth.

"I hope so. It was too lovely to pass up. And he said he would have it done and delivered to your house Saturday morning. Amazing."

There were definitely perks to this arrangement, Melissa thought, pleased with her purchase. She glanced at her watch, surprised to find it was already after noon. The shopping had flown by.

"Time to eat?" Surim asked.

"Something light would be good. Then I need to get them home."

"So Nadia can take her nap," he said, leaning close to better communicate.

Each time he did, Melissa felt an increased spark of awareness. She could get in over her head. She had to remember he was looking for a wife, not a relationship with a visiting nanny. He was leagues out of her realm. The brush of air that touched her cheeks as he spoke sent another message. She longed to lean closer. By turning her head slightly, she'd be able to touch his mouth with hers.

The thought sent flames of excitement licking through her veins, but she prudently turned her face and stepped away. Only to have Surim move closer, protecting her from being jostled by a group of rough teens laughing and shoving each other.

One of the men stepped closer to Surim and spoke rapidly. Surim shook his head.

"Are you all right?" he asked her softly.

"Fine." She smiled reassuringly at Nadia and glanced at Hamid and Alaya. For a moment she lost sight of Alaya and panicked, but before she could even voice her concern the child appeared at the far end of the stall, staring at another dress.

"If it gets more crowded, we should leave," Surim said, glancing around.

"I think we have enough outfits to carry them through several weeks. Where will we get Hamid's haircut?"

"I know a place. If you are ready, we will wind our way through the mob." Surim reached for her hand. Surely to keep her close. But his touch, as always, sent sparks of electricity coursing through her. She tried to concentrate on the children, but it was harder by the moment.

Melissa noticed the souks appeared more crowded than when they had first arrived. She admonished the older children to stay close, still grasping Nadia's small hand.

At one point Surim released her and reached for Nadia. "Let me take Nadia and you hold onto Hamid and Alaya."

Nadia smiled and looked around when Surim picked her up.

"Probably better for her to see things," Melissa said, beckoning the others. "She is so short she only had a view of knees."

Surim nodded, smiling at the little girl. He still looked a bit awkward holding her, but Melissa was pleased he'd volunteered. She'd bring them all together no matter what!

Hamid was not the quiet, docile child she'd hoped for at the barber shop. Once he realized he was the only one getting a haircut, he rebelled.

"Don't want to," he said, planting his feet and refusing to move beyond the doorway.

"You need a haircut," Melissa said, stooping down to be at his level. "Look at all the other men; they have short hair. Yours is getting scruffy, like a puppy. You don't want to look like a scruffy puppy, do you?"

Surim didn't wait for an answer, but lifted the boy and looked him in the eye.

"It is inappropriate to cause a scene in a public place. Do you understand?" His voice was firm, but not unkind.

Hamid stared at him wide-eyed and slowly nodded.

Melissa watched, knowing Surim would not severely discipline the child, glad he'd made it more of a question than command.

He set Hamid back on his feet and reached for his hand, and the two continued into the shop. The two girls had remained in the limousine with the driver. Knowing she was no longer needed, Melissa returned to the vehicle and got inside with the girls.

"Is Hamid going to be a long time?" Alaya asked, looking

up from working the puzzle they'd bought for Nadia. The two girls were on the floor of the limo putting it together. Nadia smiled as she hummed softly to herself as she tried to fit the large pieces in the wooden holder.

"Not long. Uncle Surim is with him. We'll go for lunch when they are finished, then back home for Nadia's nap. Did you like the souks?"

"They were different from shopping at home." Alaya abandoned the puzzle and moved to sit beside Melissa. "I was glad Uncle Surim was with us," she said.

"Me, too," Melissa said. She had enjoyed the excursion. She watched the entrance to the shop, waiting for him to appear with Hamid. They would have a quick lunch and then she'd take the children home while he returned to work.

Tomorrow, however, Surim would spend the entire day with her alone. She could hardly wait.

By the time they returned to the house, the children were getting rambunctious. Surim had found a restaurant that easily accommodated young children, so lunch had passed without incident. But on the ride back, Nadia had wanted to be held and had been cranky. Hamid had been in high spirits and had wanted to hurry home so he could play with his new toy. Alaya had been a bit annoyed with her siblings and had complained constantly to Melissa about the other two.

Melissa soon got them sorted out when they reached home. Nadia went straight to bed. Hamid played with his new trucks and Alaya drifted to her room, wanting to read one of her many books.

Annis asked after the expedition and Melissa relayed the highlights, then left to take a little time for herself. She walked out into the garden and headed for her favorite bench. She couldn't believe it was already February and so warm. The balmy air caressed her cheeks as she leaned back on the wooden bench to savor the peace and quiet. She was used to groups of children from the resort, but generally she'd had one age group at a time with activities suited to keep them occupied. It was more challenging to deal with three different ages and interests.

She loved caring for these children. Actually, she realized she loved them, full stop. She couldn't imagine now hard it was going to be to leave.

Or should she stay?

That might prove to be even harder. She was falling for Surim. Not that she'd ever tell anyone. But could she stay near him, seeing him every day, longing for his kisses and caresses once he was married to someone else?

Saturday dawned fair and clear. Melissa dressed in anticipation of the day she and Surim would share. She was delighted to be seeing where pearls were harvested. The fact that Surim was taking her was an added bonus. Or the highlight of the tour. One day out of time might be all she had. She'd cherish every moment!

She tried to put things in perspective. Due to her relationship to Max, Surim didn't relegate her to the nursery. She still had the guest room on the second floor. She ate most of her dinners with him. She had the run of the house, though she spent most of her time with the children.

Over the weeks she'd been in residence, she'd grown to know a lot about her employer from what he told her and from what she pieced together from the way he behaved around others. And the bits of information dropped as he compared his childhood with theirs.

She knew she shouldn't feel sorry for one of the most powerful men in the Persian Gulf area, but she did. Just a little. He hadn't had a close family. There apparently were few happy memories of his time with his parents. His best recollections always were about being at Eton. He remained friends with several boys from school. In fact, from what she could glean, he was closer to those men who still lived in England than anyone in Qu'Arim.

He also felt a strong duty to marry and produce children for the stability of his country. Yet she felt his reluctance. And anyone looking would see he was doing nothing toward that goal—instead he was spending his time with her.

It was almost nine-thirty by the time they left. Instead of the expected limo, Surim drove his own car again, as he had on her first visit to the resort site.

"How is the building coming?" she asked as they merged into traffic and began their day.

"On target so far. There have been minor mishaps, but nothing has delayed the process significantly."

"And when does it open?"

"We hope next autumn. We have a two-week window built in the construction schedule to accommodate any delays, but if anything goes beyond that we'll likely have to postpone the grand opening. Which I do not plan to do. We already have guests booked."

"Even before it's built? What are you showing for rooms and amenities?"

"We have artist renditions of the rooms, the front of the hotel, the lobby. Those have been incorporated into brochures and distributed to travel agencies around the world."

"Max is excited about opening a Bella Lucia outside of the UK,' commented Melissa. "Will he be coming back to check on things before the opening? I haven't talked with him in a while, not since the last set of translations."

"He'll fly in once more, but I shall handle things from this end. Some of the London office staff will arrive a month prior to opening to train local people to handle the day-to-day operations."

Soon, Surim turned onto the highway that flanked the sea.

The Gulf stretched out to the horizon, deep blue and calm. The breeze from the Gulf kept it from being too hot.

"It's beautiful!" Melissa exclaimed, gazing at the water. "I can't believe it's February and so warm. My mother said it was freezing in London."

"Perhaps we'll have time for a swim when we return home," he said.

"I should love that. I still can't get over being able to swim in the sea year-round."

Sometimes Surim wondered if Melissa liked him, or the location of his home. She never seemed to flirt. Did she realize how enticing she was when she challenged him? Her eyes sparkled and her laughter was infectious. Her kisses had him wanting more. Yet she never overstepped any boundaries. Was he so conceited he thought all women were after him?

He almost laughed. The only women who wanted an alliance with him were ones looking for a free ride with a wealthy man. He didn't want to believe that of Melissa.

The first pearling enterprise they came to belonged to the de Loache family, an old French family who had lived in Qu'Arim for more than a hundred years. One of their early ancestors had discovered a bed of oysters producing lovely pearls, acquired the land and launched a business renowned throughout the world.

Surim knew the owner and had arranged to have him give the tour personally. Not only for Melissa, but so Surim could discuss including tours on a regular basis as a tourist attraction exclusively from the new resort.

Claude de Loache was waiting by the long, low building when Surim drove up.

"Our host," Surim told Melissa.

In only moments, introductions had been made and Claude began to explain the different steps in pearling. Melissa was fascinated. Her attention was totally on what Claude relayed.

She asked intelligent questions and seemed to grasp all the facts quickly.

When Claude offered to take them out in one of the boats to actually see some of the oysters, she was delighted.

"If it's all right with Surim," she said.

Claude raised an eyebrow and glanced at Surim. "We bow to your wishes," he said.

Surim gave him a look. They'd known each other for many years. "It would be more than we expected, but I should like to as well."

Claude explained how they kept the oysters in beds in the sea, able to bring them up on huge flat beds using cranes. They were checked periodically to make sure everything was all right. Storms could wreak havoc, so they were especially concerned after a big one.

He had some of the men on the boat connect to the wire bed and haul it up. Dozens of oysters lay on the huge tray, water streaming off them as they were pulled from the depths. Claude reached over and took one, opening it and moving the soft foot aside. A small pearl gleamed in the sunshine.

"Too small to harvest, but doing well," he said, showing it to Melissa and Surim.

"How long before it is big enough to harvest?" she asked as he carefully replaced it on the big metal device and signaled the winch man to lower it back to the sea.

"A couple of years, probably. We have different sections of the seafloor marked for different durations. It takes a long time to make a truly beautiful pearl. We make sure no diseases sweep through, or predators. We have a continuous rotation of oysters; some are just planted, others are a year or two old and some are ready for harvesting come summer."

Surim suggested Claude consider giving tours. He suspected there would be many visitors as excited about the process as Melissa.

"Am I that transparent?" she asked, laughing. "I love every bit of information I've learned. Surim said there might be pearls to see—already harvested ones, I guess I mean."

"Indeed. In our showroom we have a large selection, some already made into jewelry, others loose to be chosen by discriminating buyers for their own particular designs."

The showroom was at the far end of the long building they'd parked beside.

Surim took her hand when helping her from the boat and seemed to forget he held it as they walked to the display area.

Melissa had no such luck forgetting. She was acutely aware of every inch of his palm against hers, of his strong fingers wrapped around her. Her arm actually seemed to tingle as they walked up the graveled path, listening to Claude explaining how he would have to change things to handle tours. Surim offered the incentive of additional buyers at the showroom. Sales meant a lot to the pearl farmer.

The showroom was elegant with thick carpeting beneath her feet and display cases and tables scattered around the large room. One wall had rows of necklaces and bracelets. Another had brooches, earrings and dinner rings.

The tables held corrugated trays with rows of loose pearls, sorted by size and color.

"This is amazing," Melissa said, transfixed by the displays.

Surim released her hand, placing it at the small of her back and urging her inside. "Wander around and see what you like. I'll talk with Claude. Take your time."

Melissa was fascinated by the wide variety of colors and sizes. One of the women at a table was sorting. She glanced up and smiled, saying something.

"I don't speak Arabic; do you speak French?" Melissa asked in that language.

The woman did. Melissa asked her what she was doing and was soon involved in learning how pearls were sorted, what made a gem-quality pearl and some of the ancient folklore about pearls.

When Melissa looked up some time later, Claude had left and Surim was leaning against the wall near the door, watching her.

"Am I taking too long?" Melissa asked, realizing how long she'd been talking with the woman.

"Not at all. I'm making mental notes about what tourists find interesting. I forget that not everyone would know about the pearl industry. And how enthralling it could be to visitors."

She smiled uncertainly.

"Did you see any you liked?"

"They are all lovely." She began to walk around the perimeter, studying the jewelry on display. Surim watched for signs of avarice, but saw none. She seemed to enjoy the pearls for their beauty, not to own them.

She finished her tour and spoke again to the woman sorting. Then she rejoined him.

"I'm ready to leave if you are."

"I thought you might buy something."

"Not today."

"Maybe I should buy you something," he suggested. Pearls against her skin would be beautiful.

"No, thank you," she said primly.

"A memento of our day together, nothing else."

"I don't think so," she said, heading for the door.

He caught her arm, stopping her.

"I can afford them, Melissa. Take them as a gift."

"I don't want you buying me pearls, Surim, and I'm not sure I want to splurge for them myself. Honestly, where would I wear pearls?"

"How about tonight? You're going to a formal reception tonight." His fingers registered the softness of her skin. She would feel like that all over, he knew. Before he got sidetracked, he let her go.

"I'll manage with the necklace I already have. It goes perfectly with the new dress."

Surim merely nodded. "Time to leave, I think." He conversed with the woman at the table in Arabic, who looked at Melissa and then at Surim and smiled. Melissa smiled back.

"What did you tell her?" she asked as they stepped out of the showroom.

"I thanked her for letting us see the lovely pearls."

When they left the pearl farm, Surim asked if she wished to see another.

"Not today. This one was perfect. I need time to absorb all the facts I've learned. Weren't they beautiful?"

He glanced at her again as he turned onto the main highway. "They are beautiful, made more so by the women who wear them."

"Tell me how long you've known M. de Loache. You sound like longtime friends, though he's a lot older, isn't he?"

"I've known Claude for many years. When I first assumed the leadership of the country, he was one of the first men to offer help however he could provide it. I would return the favor now, in increasing his business through tourism."

"Tell me about the early days. It couldn't have been easy to be a teenager taking on the leadership of an entire country. You hadn't even finished school, had you?"

Surim was silent, remembering how difficult it had been. He had not been groomed from infancy for the role, which would have made more sense. His father had not expected to die young and had felt there was time enough later to train his son. In the meantime, with factions warring within the country, he'd had other matters to attend to.

"It was difficult to deal with," was all Surim said.

"Did you ever finish school?" she asked.

"Did you think I was a dropout?"

She grinned. "Hardly, with your knowledge. But how did you go to school and run a country?"

"In the first place, most of the actual running of the country in the early days was done by the ministers. My father had chosen them well. They were good men; several remain in their positions even today. I was more a titular figurehead. So I had tutors galore. I finished basic education and then continued until I earned the equivalent of a college degree."

"Through tutors?" she asked.

"I was privileged enough to have professors from the university prepare a curriculum for me that I could follow from home. They would lecture, exam, and grade based on that."

"But no interaction with other students?"

"Very limited. When I wasn't studying calculus or world history, I was learning how to negotiate peace settlements between the warring factions in this country, and how to expand our national revenue through oil exports. There wasn't time to hang out with other students."

"Sounds lonely," she murmured.

He shrugged. "It was the way it was."

Surim didn't think often of those days. He hadn't had much choice and had gone along with the way things had turned out. He could imagine how Melissa would have handled things. She'd have found him a home, insisted he have time to grow at a normal pace and not be plunged into world affairs at the age of seventeen.

He, however, considered himself lucky the men his father had worked with had been loyal. There could have been anarchy at the time and that would have been disastrous for Qu'Arim.

CHAPTER NINE

SURIM drove to a restaurant he sometimes visited situated literally on the water. It was a floating facility anchored a short boat ride from the shore. The seafood was excellent and the ambience he knew would appeal to Melissa. She had such a sensuous feel for things. He knew she loved the flowers in the garden, not only their look and scents, but also touch. He'd seen her on more than one occasion plucking a flower and brushing it against her cheeks.

The way she pointed things out to the children in the garden, or at the shore, or even yesterday in the souks, supported her love for the natural world and her fascination with life in general.

When he reached the parking lot, she looked around with interest.

"Are we taking another boat ride?" she asked.

"To the restaurant there." He pointed to the floating structure several hundred yards from shore. From the smile that instantly appeared, he knew she approved.

"This is fantastic," she said a short time later when they were seated at one of the open windows and had placed their orders. The structure bobbed gently on the surface of the sea. The air circulating was fresh and warm. The smells coming from the kitchen were mouthwatering.

"I thought you'd like it," he murmured, watching her as she took in the quiet ambience of the place.

She smiled at him, just like the smiles she gave to Hamid and Alaya. "Surim, I have to say I'm having the time of my life today. Thank you for showing me part of your country. It's amazing."

"I'm happy to do it."

She let her smile fade slightly. "I feel guilty taking time away from your courting, though."

He was startled. "I assure you I have things well in hand." He had seen Yasine several times, and, while she sometimes bored him, he knew she'd make a suitable wife. In due time, he'd introduce her to the children and see the mutual reaction. If it went well, perhaps he'd propose within the month. But there was no rush.

Today was for himself and Melissa. It had been a long time since he'd seen Qu'Arim with fresh eyes and he was enjoying the novelty.

"Tell me about Eton. Did you ever find anything to like about England?"

"Initially, I did not. But I grew to enjoy my time in England."

"Because of Max and other friends, I bet. Didn't you miss your home?"

Surim nodded once. He had missed Qu'Arim. He had disliked the cold, wet climate of England. He had missed the familiar palm trees and native flowers. And swimming in the Gulf. He had loved his summers at home. He and Mara had been the best of friends. But he had also understood duty. His family's duty had been set long before he'd been born.

The waiter brought their lunch. Melissa tasted the fish in a light sauce and pronounced it perfect.

"It almost melts in my mouth, it's so delicate," she said.

"I am pleased you are pleased," he said.

She laughed. "Are you always so formal? Even around the children you don't seem relaxed and into playing with them. Loosen up a bit, and remember back when you were a child. I bet you were a terror. I've heard some of the stories of Max at Eton; could you have been far behind?"

Surim ate his fish, refusing to reminisce about the wilder days of his youth. They had vanished when a light plane had crashed, killing his father and mother. He could never recapture them.

"This is hardly the setting to be frivolous," he said, glancing around.

She followed suit and sobered up. "Of course, Excellency. I would expect you only to forget your role in private."

She ate her meal, gazing out over the water and virtually ignoring him. Surim felt annoyed that he'd ruined what had been a fun time. She had withdrawn and was totally polite if he asked her anything. But her spontaneity had vanished.

Melissa's enjoyment had dimmed with his comment about not being frivolous. That was what she was; she could see it. But she loved to laugh and enjoy situations. Not be formal and polite and follow protocol all the time. Much as she might fancy capturing the love of the man, she wouldn't wish to live her life like that. She embraced new experiences, always excited to learn more and see more.

This restaurant was perfect. She had never eaten on a floating one before and wished she could come another time. She was charmed that Surim had sought such a special treat for her. After the pearl farm and lunch, Melissa was sure the day couldn't get better. He hadn't said anything about the afternoon, except to suggest they might go swimming. For a moment she imagined the two of them on that beautiful stretch of beach. She'd love to be free to swim, float and generally enjoy the outing without any cares. Would he still be considering his duty?

"What are you thinking about?" he asked as he finished his meal.

She looked embarrassed. She should have kept up the conversation, not gone off in some daydream.

"Actually I was wondering if we were still going to the

beach later. I haven't had a proper swim myself since I've been here because I'm usually watching the children."

"We will go by the resort and then head for home. If we are very quiet, we can slip in, change and be gone before they know we're there."

She'd suspected he'd been more carefree before the responsibilities of his office pressed down. This sounded like fun.

"You're on. You really think we can do that?"

Surim smiled slyly. "I know a secret way into the house."

Melissa was enchanted. "A secret passage! Where is it?"

"I cannot tell you; you'll have to trust me."

She opened her mouth to protest, then closed it. "I do." She laughed, feeling lighthearted once again. And crashing head over heels for a man who put duty before all else. Was it her destiny to fall for unsuitable men?

After they ate, Surim drove them to the resort site. "I like to check on it each day," he said.

The outside walls had been framed. The floor joists for the second and third stories were in place, ladders leaning against them to allow workers easy access. Only a handful of workers were there. It was Saturday, and she knew Qu'Arim followed normal work weeks of Monday through Friday.

"I can see the shape better now," she said, looking from the car. "It's going to be beautiful, isn't it? I love the arched windows and the airy feeling of the high ceilings. Like at your house, right?"

"Similar. We want to incorporate our distinctive architecture to enhance the visitors' feeling of being in a different place than they normally go. We are extending the feeling to the entire layout, emphasizing the Arabian mystique and minimizing the western style that they see all over Europe."

"It will be fabulous."

"Max and his family will be here for the grand opening. You'll have to join us all for the event," Surim said.

They walked to the restaurant. The outer walls with their soaring windows facing the Gulf were completed. Inside they were plastering and incorporating mosaic tiles on the floors and part way up the two side walls. The designs were geometric and quite intricate. Surim led her toward the back where the kitchen had been laid out. None of the appliances were yet in place, but electrical wiring had been pulled and plumbing put in.

"It'll be much like the one I saw in Mayfair. Are you following their design?" she asked.

"It's Max's design that we're following. Come, let's see how far they have come on the lobby."

They explored for another half hour, remaining on the ground floor. Surim voted against their using ladders to see the upper levels. "Time enough when the stairs are in," he said.

Melissa complied, but she knew if he'd been on his own, without her, he would not have hesitated to climb up and see the progress. They walked out of the lobby and she looked around.

"Even before the landscaping is put in, it's gorgeous." There were several palm trees that had been worked around. And the view of the blue water stretching out before them was enough to satisfy even the most demanding tourist. "This is going to be a wonderful place for people to visit," she said.

"I hope so. It's been a dream of mine for a long time. I'm glad to see it come to fruition. If you have seen enough, we'll return home."

Home, a place to live and love. Melissa smiled and headed back for the car, knowing for however long she was to live in Qu'Arim, his house was truly home.

Surim drove the car to the back of the villa, into a multi-bay garage. He helped Melissa from the vehicle, and put one finger to his lips.

"Shh, now," he admonished.

She almost laughed. She had never seen a playful side to the man before and found it enchanting.

He took her hand and went to the side of the garage, peering around the edge of the building. Satisfied they were alone, he hurried across the stretch of lawn to the side of the house. Here he stayed close to the wall, slipping behind some shrubbery at one point. There was a small door.

"It's really a secret entrance," she whispered.

"Not so secret; the staff use it," he said.

"Don't tell me that. To me it's a secret way known only to a few. Where does it go?"

"Into a hallway that goes between the servants' quarters and the reception room. Come, quietly now. I hope we don't run into the children exploring."

"You know they do that?"

"Of course." He eased open the door and slipped inside, tugging her behind him. The illumination was dim when the door closed behind them, but Surim knew where he was going. He walked quietly toward the front of the house, entering the reception room in only a moment.

"Now's the tricky part. Here's the plan. We get to our rooms, change and meet back here in less than ten minutes. Can you do that?"

Melissa stifled a giggle, her eyes bright with laughter. "Aye, sir, no problem, unless the kids are out and about."

"That's why we have to be fast."

He eased the door to the main foyer open a crack and peeped through it.

Melissa almost held her breath. Was there someone out there? Finally Surim flung the door wide open and began to walk quickly across to the stairs. She almost had to run to keep up with his longer stride.

In her room, she let the laughter out as she hurried to find her bathing suit and cover-up. She hadn't had that much fun in a long time. She changed swiftly and grabbed a clean towel from her en suite bath. She slipped into sandals and headed for the door before she noticed the empty wrapping paper on the bed. She went to the closet. Her new dress was hanging there. Glad it had arrived as promised, she could hardly wait for evening.

Just then she heard what sounded like a thundering herd of elephants. Oh, no, it was the children.

She went to the door to listen. They seemed to be running toward the stairs to the nursery. Maybe Annis had taken them for a walk and they were now returning. She waited a moment after the last sound, then opened her door an inch. Peering into the hall, she saw it was deserted.

Quickly she closed her door behind her and lightly ran down the stairs. In less than a minute she was in the reception room, trying to catch her breath and not laugh aloud.

Surim followed a moment later. His eyes sparkled and there was definitely an air of relaxation about the man Melissa didn't remember seeing. She was so glad he'd asked her out for the day. It was her best day off ever!

They reached the white sand beach in only a few moments, slipping from the secret door and crossing the gardens in a circuitous route designed to foil anyone trying to follow them.

"I feel like a spy in a novel," Melissa said when they reached the beach. "I almost expect our escape submarine to be waiting just off shore." She looked toward the buoy. "I think I see the periscope!"

"And where will it take us?"

"Good question. I can't imagine any place more perfect than this one," she said, walking on the hot sand. She couldn't wait to plunge into the water and swim to her heart's content without having to worry about children on the shore.

She shed her cover-up near the water's edge and ran into the warm sea. She began swimming toward the buoy, not in a race but just to enjoy the sensation. In a moment Surim came up on her right.

"Did you want to race?" he asked.

"No, I'll leave that to you and Alaya. I'm just going to enjoy myself." She kept steadily heading for the marker. He kept pace beside her. When they reached it, she treaded water while Surim dove deep. A moment later he resurfaced and dove again. Then he brought up a lovely shell, which he handed to her.

"It's not a pearl, but another gift from the sea," he said gravely.

"It's lovely." She'd treasure it forever, more than a pearl or other jewelry she could get, because it came from Surim. The perfect shell was faintly pink on the inside, with even white ridges on the outside. It fit in the palm of her hand.

"The shells out here are more intact. Once a storm washes them to the shore, they get broken or chipped," he said.

They paddled around the deep water for a while until Melissa began to get tired. She swam back to shore slowly, savoring the feel of the water caressing her skin, the sun warm on her back.

She spread out her towel and lay down to let the sun dry the water clinging to her skin. Surim was still swimming. It was peaceful without the children. Not that she didn't enjoy every minute with them.

"You will burn if you stay long in the sun," Surim said.

She opened her eyes a slit and looked at him. When had he come out of the water to lie down beside her? Had she dozed off?

His fingertips brushed against her shoulder. "You are already getting pink."

"The bane of my life." She sighed and sat up. Fumbling for her cover-up, she tried to ignore the sensations that tingled down her arm from his touch. Impossible. She could only hope she looked unaffected.

"Your skin is beautiful; you do not wish to mar it."

Her breath caught and she couldn't speak. Closing her eyes, Melissa savored the sound of his voice, deep and rich. She wished they had the chance to explore the attraction she felt around him. But their worlds were too distant. He was getting married soon, and one day she'd return to England.

"I have to get back," she said, opening her eyes and gathering her things. "I want to have a nice hot bath and take my time getting ready for tonight." It was a lame excuse, but the only thing she could think up. Who in the world would take four hours to get ready?

He held out his hand to help her up and she placed hers in his. He brought her to her feet effortlessly. The warm expanse of chest in front of her tantalized. She wished she dared brush her fingertips across that skin, feel the heat and texture. She looked and her gaze locked with his. She felt as if she'd been touched, though there was still a good ten inches between them. His dark eyes hid mysteries she'd love to explore. His lips were sculpted and hers began to ache with longing to touch them again, to feel their warmth against her skin. Her breathing became erratic.

She had to get away or do something so foolish she'd be sent away instantly.

"Thank you for a wonderful day," she said, then turned and walked as fast as she could back to the house.

Thankfully, Surim didn't catch up.

Surim stood on the beach and watched her hurry away. For a moment he considered going after her. But didn't move. The sensations that swirled around them startled him. He knew better than to attribute them to anything but sex. Melissa was so sexy it made him ache. But she was also a guest in his house. One, moreover, who had personal ties to a longtime friend. He would do nothing to dishonor her or that relationship.

He'd wanted to kiss her but had been afraid a single kiss wouldn't be enough. He needed his emotions under better control before unleashing the desire that flared whenever he thought about her. He'd love to kiss her until she moaned with pleasure. Touch that soft skin all over. Make love to her far into the night.

Turning with an oath, he plunged back into the sea. Swimming to the buoy and beyond would cool the ardor.

Tonight he'd make sure she had a good time at the British Consulate, and then tomorrow take care to keep his distance.

He had a wife to find.

The thought was even more depressing than usual.

When it was time to leave that evening, Surim made a trip to the nursery. It felt strange to stop off before leaving, but he hadn't seen the children all day, and he wanted to check in on them before they went to bed.

"Excellency," Annis said when he entered.

Hamid and Alaya were playing a board game. Nadia was lying on the large chair, holding her blanket close.

"I came to see the children. They have been no problem today?"

"They have been easy to manage, though missing Melissa. I spent part of the morning reviewing what they've learned in Arabic."

"Very good."

He went to the small table where Alaya and Hamid played. "Good game?"

"She's beating me," Hamid complained.

"You won last time," Alaya commented, smiling up at Surim. "But I am the better player, probably because I'm older, right, Uncle Surim?"

"Most likely. But it isn't so much who wins, or how often, as how much fun you two have when playing."

"Well said." Melissa spoke from the doorway.

"Melissa!" The two jumped up from the table and ran to her.

Surim couldn't take his eyes off her. The long dress fitted her perfectly, subtly accentuating every curve, and the deep green of the silk brought out the sparkling green of her eyes and made her creamy skin, now tinged with gold after days out in the sun, look luminous. Quite simply, she looked incredible.

"Oh, you look so beautiful," Alaya said.

"Are you going out tonight?" Hamid asked. "I thought you'd spend it with us. I missed you today."

"I missed all of you today. Tomorrow we'll have a great time together, but tonight I'm going out with Uncle Surim. To a reception at the British Consulate."

Nadia struggled up from the chair and walked to Surim, forcing his attention from Melissa. "I'm tired," she said, holding up her arms to be picked up.

He scooped her up and looked at her. "Did you take a nap today?"

She nodded.

"Did you play hard?"

She nodded again.

"Then you have a right to be tired. Annis can put you to bed now if you want."

He looked at Annis, who came to take the toddler.

"She usually stays up until seven-thirty, but I can put her down now. I think she has a touch of sunburn from playing in the garden today," Annis said.

Melissa came over, her gown whispering softly as she moved, and brushed the back of her fingers against her rosy cheeks. "She does feel warm. Were they long in the sun?" she said in French.

Annis shook her head.

"Good night, baby girl. I'll see you in the morning."

Nadia snuggled against Annis's neck and closed her eyes. Surim was surprised. He knew Nadia was not as fond of Annis as she was of Melissa. Tonight she seemed listless. Maybe she had played too much trying to keep up with her older siblings.

After giving the other children a hug and kiss goodbye, Melissa was ready to leave. Surim bade them goodnight and ushered her from the room.

"I didn't expect to find you there," she said as they descended the stairs together. "But I was glad."

"As you point out on many occasions, they are my responsibilities."

"They're more than that. They're your family."

"Before we go," he said at the foot of the stairs, "I have something for you."

He withdrew the pearl necklace from his pocket and dangled it from his fingers.

"Oh, Surim, no." She gazed at the strand, a frown on her face. "I told you not to buy me any."

"Humor me, Melissa. Take this as a token from the children. A reminder of Qu'Arim wherever you may go in life."

"I can't."

"Yes." He unfastened the strand and encircled her neck, hooking it at the back. "They go perfectly with your dress. You look very beautiful tonight."

"Thank you." She brushed her fingertips over the pearls. "They feel cool."

"They will warm with your skin." He studied her with the pearls. Their color was perfect against her skin. They gleamed in the light.

"Take off the other necklace; I don't want to wear both. And thank you. Thank you very much," she said at last, turning to present her back so he could unfasten the gold chain.

"Where's the nearest mirror?" she asked.

"In the salon."

Surim watched her walk to the mirror and look at the new necklace. He was satisfied with her radiant smile.

The British Consulate glittered with lights and music as they entered. Surim received preferential treatment and Melissa as his escort accompanied him. They bypassed those waiting in the receiving line to meet the new Consulate and were swept to the front of the line, stepping in behind an elderly lady and her escort.

Melissa was thrilled to meet George Farmingham, the representative of England to Qu'Arim—especially when he asked her to promise him a few moments later in the evening as he'd like a fellow countryman's opinion of the country.

"So will you rave about our country?" Surim asked quietly in her ear when they moved on.

She smiled up at him. "What do you think?"

They entered the large reception hall. Surim nodded to acquaintances and exchanged greetings with others.

"Your Excellency," a soft voice said to his left.

Melissa peeped around him to see a petite young woman a few years older than she smiling diffidently at Surim. She wore a beautiful teal-blue gown, and her hair was shot through with pearls, their pale white color like sparkling moon drops in her dark hair. Melissa felt a spurt of jealousy when Surim smiled at her.

"Yasine, I did not know you were to be here."

"My father was invited and my mother was indisposed, so I came with him." She looked at Melissa, her friendly expression remaining. "We have not met, I believe."

"Yasine, this is my friend from England, Melissa Fox. Melissa, Yasine bin Shora. She was a friend of Mara's."

"How do you do?" Melissa said. Her heart sank. This was one of the women Surim had referred to as a candidate for his wife. She was truly beautiful and seemed sweet as well.

"I visited Mara in England several times over the years. I miss her dreadfully," she said, her smile fading as she thought about her friend.

"Melissa is helping with Mara's children. You must come some day and visit with them."

"I should love to," Yasine said. "I have not seen Nadia since she was a baby. Has she grown as pretty as Alaya?"

"Yes," Surim said.

"We have not spoken much about the children. How are you coping with instant fatherhood?" Yasine asked.

Melissa listened, glad Yasine was bowing to convention and speaking English at the Consulate. She and Surim could have had this conversation in Arabic. It was interesting she mentioned their not speaking about the children. Had they had numerous conversations recently? Yasine must have been the reason for Surim's late nights earlier in the week.

"With Melissa's help, I'm beginning to get to know them better. Children are a mystery to me."

Yasine laughed. Melissa had to admit the woman had charm and looks. She'd make a perfect match to Surim's own handsome features. And she seemed genuinely interested in the children.

"I suspect you are of the mind that children should be handled by the women in the household," Yasine said. "Yet my father was very involved with me and my brothers when we were young. I think we have a close relationship because of it."

One that Surim had lacked with his own father, Melissa thought. Yet neither of her companions voiced that thought. Had he shared that with Yasine? Melissa wondered. For a moment the special bond she thought between them faded. Any confidences he'd shared had to do with the children, not some regard for her. How foolish could one woman be?

A waiter circulated carrying a tray with beverages. She took one, sipping the cold liquid, wishing she could melt away into the crowd and see if there were any other British citizens present she could talk to.

Before she could say anything, however, the new Consulate came over.

"Ah, there you are, Your Excellency, Miss Fox. I believe I have met everyone invited here tonight and I am following up on talking with Miss Fox."

She was amazed he had remembered her name.

"Sir," she said, wondering what someone called a Consulate. Was there a special title?

"Do you mind if I steal her away for a short time?" George Farmingham asked after being introduced to Yasine.

"I brought her to circulate and see if she would find others from England here. Melissa is staying at my home and will be in our country for some time. I hope she finds friends," Surim said.

"Excellent, come with me, my dear, and we'll see what compatriots we can locate."

Melissa left with the friendly older man, ignoring the pang she felt leaving Surim with Yasine. But it was nothing to what might be in store, so she'd best get used to it.

Soon she had met a dozen UK expatriates living in Qu'Arim and loving it. One couple invited her over to visit on her next free day. A young man working in the tourist industry commented on the resort and she told him a bit about Bella Lucia going in, and the progress of the site. He asked if she'd be able to get hold of an invitation for him to see it before it opened.

George Farmingham seemed pleased to meet so many British citizens and suggested keeping in touch.

Melissa and the others had begun throwing out suggestions for a monthly get-together when she recognized one of Surim's aides approach him to speak to him. Surim looked over at her a moment later and immediately headed her way.

"Excuse me, Mr Farmingham. I need Melissa," he said when he reached their group.

"Of course. Do join us when you can, my dear," the man said, turning back to continue his conversation with the others.

"What is it?" Melissa asked.

"We have to leave. I just got word from Annis that Nadia is very ill."

CHAPTER TEN

"WHAT? What happened?" Melissa asked as she swiftly followed Surim to the entrance where the limo was already waiting.

He delayed answering until they were in the car and speeding away.

"Annis said she is vomiting and her fever has spiked to one hundred and three and she has diarrhea. I suspect her warmth from earlier wasn't from sunburn but from fever."

"Oh, dear. Poor baby." Melissa lapsed into silence, reviewing all her experience with sick children, and her training. Dehydration was a worry with Nadia's symptoms, especially since she was so little. What could be wrong with her? Were the others sick as well? She longed to hold the child close and comfort her. Couldn't the car go any faster?

Despite the minutes seeming to crawl by, they reached Surim's home in short order. Scarcely had the car stopped before Melissa was out and running into the house and up the stairs. Surim was right beside her.

She burst into the nursery to find Annis holding Nadia, rocking her. The little girl was pink with heat and listlessly lying against Annis's shoulder. She roused slightly when she saw Melissa and called her name.

"Sweetie, I'm here. I came as soon as I heard." She

scooped her up and held her close, resting her cheek against Nadia's forehead.

"Oh, Surim, she's burning up. I think we should take her to hospital and have a doctor look at her."

"I also," Annis said. "This is more than just an upset tummy."

"Come, we'll go straight away," he said, turning, his arm around Melissa's shoulders as if to lend support.

"Wait, where's her blanket? She'll want something familiar," Melissa said.

"Here." Annis brought it from the rocker. She patted the toddler's back and said something in Arabic.

"I hope that was a blessing," Melissa said as they hurried down the stairs. She had to move more slowly than she wished due to her long dress and high-heeled shoes while holding the child.

"It was. Do you want me to carry her?"

"It might be easier," Melissa said at the bottom of the stairs to the nursery. But when she went to hand her to Surim, Nadia clung and began to cry.

"Okay, baby, there, there, you're fine. You stay right here with me," she said, hugging her again, giving Surim a quick shake of her head.

"Just don't fall," he said, holding her elbow as they descended the main stairs.

In only moments they were heading for the inner city and one of the best hospitals in Qu'Arim.

It didn't take the doctors long to diagnose Nadia's illness.

"Meningitis? Where would she have got meningitis?" Melissa asked, stunned.

Surim looked at her. "Did you take her someplace recently? Was she exposed to crowds?"

"Except for the souks and the restaurant Friday, we haven't been anywhere since I arrived, except the beach and grounds. Oh, Surim, she's so little to be this sick."

He reached out and captured her hand with his, squeezing slightly and drawing her closer as he spoke with the doctor. The little girl was gravely ill. They immediately put her on an IV for fluids and medication. She was being taken to Intensive Care.

"I want to go with her," Melissa said at one point, not understanding a word the doctor was saying, but determined not to leave Nadia alone where she'd be frightened.

Surim spoke to the doctor and the man nodded.

"We can stay with her. She'll have a private room and full-time nurse. Do you want to go home first and change?"

"No, I want to be with her right now. Is she awake?"

"He says she is asleep and will be in her room in a couple of minutes."

The doctor spoke at length again and Surim nodded. The doctor bowed slightly and left.

"What was that last bit? More bad news?"

"Bacterial meningitis is highly contagious. You and I need shots, as does anyone in the household who has been around Nadia. I am having a doctor go to the house to inoculate everyone. Let's hope Alaya and Hamid don't come down with this. Once we have our shots, we'll be permitted to go to her room."

In less than twenty minutes Melissa and Surim entered the private room. A nurse looked up at their arrival and Surim spoke rapidly in Arabic. Melissa scarcely noticed; she rushed to the bed.

Nadia looked so tiny in the hospital crib. There was an IV drip into her left arm, the needle taped into place. She opened her eyes when Melissa arrived and held out her arms.

Wrapping her in the blanket, Melissa eased her from the crib, Surim helping to keep the tube untangled. She sat on the chair and cuddled Nadia close.

"There, sweetie, we're here. You're going to be fine."

She held her for several minutes and gradually Nadia grew quiet and sleepy.

"This place needs a rocking chair," she said, rocking back and forth with the toddler.

"I shall see to it," Surim said, hovering over the two of them.

"She's going to be all right, isn't she?" Melissa asked in French. She knew meningitis was especially deadly with the old and the young. She didn't want to even think about Nadia not recovering. But if she had to hear bad news, she didn't want Nadia to also hear it.

"It will be some hours before the doctor knows for sure," Surim said. He dragged another chair over and reached out to caress Nadia's cheek. "I didn't realize how tiny she is. When she's running around, she's so full of energy. Then, suddenly, this."

"It did come on fast, but I think that's expected for this disease. So there's someone else in this city who has this illness. Do you have a public health system to warn citizens? What about the other children?"

"It is taken care of. Now we have to concentrate on getting this child well."

Surim admired Melissa's composure. He could do no less, but the fear that grew inside was hard to contain. He brushed the child's soft cheek and felt the heat. She seemed smaller than her two years. And so precious. When had he fallen in love with Mara's children? He knew he'd never be the same if something happened to her.

Yet he felt totally powerless to do anything. He hated the feeling. He had the entire country at his disposal, yet the doctor said all was being done that could be. Nature and the antibiotics they were giving her would have to take their course.

He wanted guarantees. He wanted to know this child would survive, thrive and grow into a beautiful woman as her mother had been.

"How do parents stand it?" he murmured.

"What?" Melissa turned to look at him. She was so close. Her beautiful face was drawn with worry. Her eyes haunted.

He wanted to comfort her, but lacked the words.

"Deal with sickness with their children. I feel so helpless."

"Me, too. I guess it's just part of life. But it's hard, isn't it? This is my first experience with a serious illness, though I had training for it. At a resort, children are rarely sick, except for tummy aches for overindulging." She bit her lip, looking back at Nadia. "She's been through a lot for two years of life. I'm hoping she's strong enough to beat this."

"She is. She has to be!"

Melissa gave a soft smile and reached out to grasp his hand. "From your lips to God's ear," she said.

The hours dragged by slowly. At one point Surim persuaded Melissa to replace the sleeping child in the crib to give her arms a rest.

He asked the nurse to bring in a rocking chair. He called his aide and made sure he had things covered. Surim also instructed him to have the inoculation, and then make sure everyone at the house complied. He also told him to bring a change of clothing for both of them.

He called Annis to speak with her, telling her what Nadia had, and warning her to downplay the severity with the other children. He did not want them upset any more than necessary.

Melissa's eyes were gritty with lack of sleep. But she was afraid to doze off for fear Nadia would need her. She felt fearful the child would not respond to the medication. Or there would be lasting problems caused by the disease. How could she have left her tonight for a party when Nadia had needed her? She rose again and leaned over the crib, rearranging the light covers, hoping the child would wake up feeling better.

Surim came back into the hospital room.

"Any change?" he asked.

Melissa shook her head. She straightened and looked at him, wanting more than he could give.

"The doctor said there wouldn't be for a while; I was hopeful, however. They are doing all they can," he said, looking at the little girl.

"You say that often enough and I'll believe it," she said crossly. "Why can't they cure her instantly?"

"That's what I want as well."

"Surim, what if she doesn't get better?" Melissa asked on a whisper. "I couldn't bear that."

He reached out and pulled her into his arms. "She will get well, Melissa. I won't accept anything else."

Startled, Melissa gave a choked gurgle of laughter at the thought of Surim ordering the disease away. The laughter quickly dissolved into tears. She was so afraid for Nadia.

Surim's embrace tightened, trying to give her courage and hope by his presence. She relished the steady beat of his heart, the strength of his arms. She couldn't imagine spending this watch alone. What if the child had been in a boarding school, thousands of miles away from anyone who cared.

"Melissa?"

"She's so little."

"She'll be fine; we have to hold onto that thought."

She nodded, brushing her tears and looking up at him.

He brushed another lonely tear away from her cheek, then leaned closer and kissed her.

His lips against hers broke something loose inside. She wrapped her arms around his neck and kissed him back, pouring out the feelings she kept hidden. She loved this man. She knew they would never share a future together, but for tonight, being together in this hospital room, sharing the vigil, was enough. She'd draw from his strength and go on once Nadia was out of danger.

He ended the kiss far too soon for her. But only a second

later a nurse entered carrying a rocking chair. Had he heard her footsteps in the hall?

Melissa stepped away quickly. She could not bear to have adverse gossip circulate because of his comforting gesture. And that was all it was, for comfort. She appreciated his efforts. At least, for a few startling moments, it had taken her mind off Nadia's illness.

Once the nurse had checked the baby and left, Surim turned to Melissa.

"I'm glad you're here with me for this. I just wish she'd wake up and be fit again."

"Me, too," she said, leaning against him as he encircled her shoulders and the two of them watched the sick little girl.

Nadia, however, was slow to respond to the drugs. The next day passed with nurses and doctors watching her closely. Melissa changed into comfortable clothes brought from home. She rarely left the toddler's side, holding her when she was awake, watching her closely while she slept.

Surim was there longer than she'd expected. He left for a couple of hours in the afternoon, returning in time to spell her for a meal. He insisted she go outside and walk around the building if nothing else.

"I don't want you dropping from exhaustion. Then where would we be?" he asked.

"What about you?"

"I had exercise, and checked on the other children. They are worried about you and Nadia."

"Me?"

"In light of their parents' deaths, any prolonged absence is suspect," he explained.

"Of course. But I can't leave Nadia."

"Tonight, once she's asleep, I think it best if we both return home for an hour or two to reassure Hamid especially. I'd hate for him to have nightmares again."

"I don't want to leave her."

"You will do her no service if you get ill yourself. And the other children want to see you."

Melissa took a breath. He was right. And she worried about the others. She wanted to make sure they weren't coming down with meningitis too. "Very well." And maybe Nadia would be on the road to recovery by the time she saw Alaya and Hamid.

The two older children rushed to greet Melissa and Surim when they arrived home. They had been sitting on the stairs waiting for them.

"I thought you'd gone away," Hamid said, hugging Melissa.

"No, sweetie, just staying at the hospital with Nadia."

"Is she going to die?" Alaya asked.

"No." Melissa refused to consider that.

"Can we see her?"

"When she's well again, we'll bring her home and you'll all be together again," Melissa promised, hoping that would be sometime very soon.

"And how do you two feel?" Surim asked.

"I'm fine. Annis said my appetite is like a camel," Hamid boasted.

Melissa laughed. "I'm so glad to hear that. And you, Alaya?"

"I miss Nadia. When is she coming home?"

"We don't know that yet. But she's getting the best care at the hospital."

Alaya didn't look convinced.

"Come into the salon and we'll tell you all we know," Surim suggested, holding out his hand to Hamid.

The four of them soon settled on the sofa, the two children between the two adults.

"Mummy and Daddy went to hospital before they died," Hamid said gravely.

"Yes, but most of the time staying in a hospital gets people well. Nadia will get better and be home before you know it," Surim said gently.

"I know it now and she's not home," Alaya said. "Can we go see her?"

"Not just yet. When she's better, we'll see if that will be permitted."

Melissa was so tired she wanted to lie down and go to sleep for a week. But she knew they had to reassure these children and then she had to go back to the hospital. She was still too worried about Nadia to leave her for long. The toddler was not yet out of danger. And Melissa was afraid she'd wake up and not see a familiar face by her bed.

After spending time with the children, and putting them to bed, Surim took Melissa back to the hospital.

"I'm sure they will be fine. Annis will watch them carefully," he said in response to her worry about Alaya and Hamid.

"Physically, sure. But you saw how much reassurance they needed. I feel so torn."

"I don't think they'll stop worrying about Nadia until she's home."

"Which I do hope will be soon."

Melissa felt his warm, strong hand briefly squeeze hers, and she closed her eyes. He was trying to comfort her. Just as she was certain he'd meant to do when he'd kissed her at the hospital. Only she hadn't reacted as if it was comfort. Desire had spiked. Yearning for more than a brief embrace had flared. She had fallen in love with the man and he hadn't a clue. He was planning to marry a *suitable* woman from his own culture and Melissa was destined to be on the outside forever.

Only, she wasn't sure she could do that anymore. His kisses had unlocked something wild and demanding. She wanted more, and if she couldn't have it she wasn't strong enough to stay and watch him marry another woman and bring her to the lovely house by the sea. She couldn't bear to take care of his children when she suddenly wanted to have his children herself.

A darling little boy with dark eyes like his father. And, hopefully, a girl with long black hair, who would wrap Surim around her little finger just as Nadia had done.

Yet could she bear to leave Alaya, Hamid and Nadia? She loved those children. She'd had no idea working for a family would be so vastly different from her childcare position at the resort. There she'd made friends with children, but none had stayed beyond two weeks. She remembered different ones fondly, but none with the love she had for Surim's wards.

"We're here," Surim said a moment later.

Melissa blinked and looked around. He had parked in the car park next to the hospital. The journey had flown by.

"Are you sure you should be here tonight? You could stay home. I'll call if there is any change," he said, but Melissa shook her head.

"I need to be with her. She's so tiny. What if she awoke and we weren't there?"

"I'll be here. It's not as if she'd awake to strangers."

"You're staying?"

"Of course. Nadia is my own. I'm as worried about her as you are."

He reached out a hand and cradled her jaw and cheek. "But I'm also worried about you." He brushed his thumb beneath her eye. "You look so tired."

Her heart rate increased exponentially at his touch, at his words. Try as she might to remain rational, hope blossomed. "I am, and I'm worried. But I couldn't sleep at home. I need to be with her," she said firmly.

For a moment he gazed into her eyes, before leaning over and brushing his lips against hers.

"Then let's go see how our girl is doing."

Nadia was still sleeping. According to the nurse, she had not stirred while they'd been gone.

Surim checked on her while Melissa watched, seeing the difference in him from when she'd first arrived. When she left, she'd go knowing the children had made a place for themselves with Surim. He wouldn't send them away to a school. They had gradually formed a strong bond of love. Melissa wanted to be thankful for that, but she felt the happiness she'd known these last weeks slipping away. She didn't want to leave, but she couldn't stay.

About ten-thirty Nadia woke up. She was fretful, but sipped some juice and the nurse was pleased with that. Another round of tests followed. It was almost midnight by the time Melissa sat in the rocking chair and held the child. She still ran a high fever, but was kept hydrated by the IV. She was listless, which was so unlike her. Melissa rocked her gently, wishing she could send good health through osmosis.

Yasine tapped quietly on the open door. She was dressed as if for a party in a silk suit and pearls. She rushed into the room to Surim, who rose as she reached him.

"Oh, Surim, I just found out when I was at a dinner party tonight and had my driver come immediately." She looked at Nadia, cuddled with Melissa. "How is she? What distressing news."

"She is still quite sick." He escorted Yasine from the room. "Meningitis can be contagious; you should not be in the room."

Melissa didn't hear any more, except the low murmur of voices in the hall. She rested her head against Nadia's and continued rocking. She appreciated the woman's instant response. She would undoubtedly make a good mother for the children.

When Nadia fell asleep some time later, Melissa put her back in the crib. Surim still had not returned. Had he escorted Yasine home? She paced the room trying to work out the kinks from sitting so long in the rocking chair. When she went to the window, all she saw was darkness. The grounds of the hospital were not lit up this late. Still she gazed out into the night. The stars were bright in the sky. She wished she were in the garden at Surim's home. Enjoying the peaceful night—and with no worries.

"Melissa?" He had entered without her hearing him.

She turned.

"You need to get some rest," he said, crossing the room to her side. His hands came to her shoulders to massage away some of the tension.

She looked at the little girl in the crib, rather than look into Surim's eyes. He couldn't see her feelings, could he? She'd be mortified if he suspected. But every fiber of her being longed to sink in against him, absorb some of his strength.

When his hands moved up to her neck and then threaded in her hair, she almost moaned with pleasure. He tilted her head slightly and she looked into his dear familiar eyes, her heart catching.

He narrowed his own gaze and stared into her eyes. "I want to kiss you again."

A sweet smile came involuntarily. "I should like that above all things," she said simply. She was too tired to dissemble tonight. She already knew she had to leave. What would one more kiss hurt?

It didn't hurt at all; it was glorious. His mouth moved against hers, gently at first, then with more passion. Opening her lips, he deepened the kiss, bringing her fully against him as his hand slipped from her head to her back, pulling her against him. She angled her head slightly to better kiss him back.

Endless waves of enchantment swept through her. She wanted more yet would have to settle for this. Sadly, she gently withdrew from the kiss. She would treasure these memories her whole life, but she was realistic enough to know when to stop.

He rested his forehead against hers, his eyes dark and dangerous.

"I was not ready to stop," he said softly.

She smiled sadly. "Me either."

"Then why?"

She pulled away and went to the crib. "Surim, you are looking for a wife. Anything between us keeps you from that goal."

"I'm not married yet."

"No, but you will be. And I can't stay. I need to return to England."

"Stay with me, raise my children."

To see him for the next eighteen or twenty years? Watch him with his own children, and his cousin's? Have to see him with Yasine and know she wanted him for herself? She absolutely could not do that!

"The children have responded so well to your care. Hamid hasn't had a nightmare in weeks. They are learning Arabic and doing well with their English schooling. And they've even accepted me. You can't leave," he said urgently.

She was torn. The sincerity in his tone convinced her he wanted her to stay. But things were too difficult. She could not do it. Slowly she shook her head.

He was silent for a long moment, then in a calm voice he said, "Then you must be my wife, Melissa. I choose you to marry me."

CHAPTER ELEVEN

MELISSA looked at him in shock. Surim wanted to marry her? For a blinding second her heart swelled in joy. Then reality took hold. He didn't love her. He didn't believe in love. He was worried she'd leave and he'd have to find someone else to help Annis with the children. Had that been the reasons for his kisses, his taking her out? To keep her happy enough to stay and make the children's lives easier?

"I can't marry you," she said, stepping away, feeling sick at the thoughts that crowded her mind. If anyone had told her earlier that she'd refuse an offer of marriage from Surim, she'd have thought them crazy. But now, with no word of love, with no reason except he didn't like the idea of her leaving the children, how could she even think of accepting?

"It would be the perfect solution," he said reasonably. "The children love you. They've had enough disruption in their lives without another. You like Qu'Arim, at least the parts you've seen. And we get along fine."

"Oh, right, that's a great recommendation for a lifelong commitment to live together. I'm sorry, Surim, but my answer is no. And I think it best if I leave as soon as Nadia is well."

"No, I want you to stay!"

"This makes it awkward," she said, trying to remain stead-fast in her resolve, but weakening by the moment. To be married to the man she loved, without being loved in return, would mean nothing but heartbreak.

"I know you like the children. Would being married to me be so difficult?" he asked, ducking his head so his eyes were on a level with hers.

She shook her head. "Surim, we aren't suited. We're from different backgrounds—oh, wow, is that an understatement."

He captured her shoulders, turning her to face him. "I was also raised in England, for the most part. More of my formative years were spent there than here. I have a job—it just happens to encompass leading a country—so you can say I work for my living. You know I need to marry to produce heirs. Don't you long for children of your own? You are so good with them, I'd think you'd like to have a houseful."

She stared into his warm brown eyes and yearned to have a little boy who would have those same eyes.

"You don't believe in love," she blurted out.

"We have discussed that issue before. Look at the longevity of marriages in my country. They function well without love. And affection grows. We would have a wonderful life together."

Pictures of the two of them at formal dinners and receptions flashed into her mind. Then with children, Melissa always taking care of them and after him to spend more time at home, to share in their lives before they were grown and gone. Or sitting alone in the salon waiting for him to return late at night and having a few words before bed.

Where was the vision of confidences shared, of plans made, of family time? Or couple time? She couldn't imagine it.

"I want more than affection," she said finally. "I want to be loved and cherished. I want to be more than a mother to a houseful of children. I want to be a partner and confidante and lover. I want it all. I don't want only a part of it."

Maybe she should think it over longer, consider all the ramifications. But her instincts were good and she knew she needed more in a marriage than what Surim offered, much as she longed to say yes.

"Thank you for the honor you offered me," she said, dropping her gaze lest she be swayed. "I appreciate it more than you know."

"But the answer remains no," he said softly.

She nodded.

He brushed a kiss on her cheek and released her, turning.

"If you have things in hand here, I'll return home and check up on the other children. I'll be back early in the morning," he said, already walking toward the door. He paused and looked at her.

"If anything changes with Nadia, have them call me immediately."

"I will." She held her breath until he left, then let the tears flood her eyes.

Was she a total idiot, refusing an offer of marriage from the man she loved? Giving away her chance to stay with children she loved? To have little ones of her own.

Confused, hurt and lonely, Melissa returned to the rocking chair. She had a lot of thinking to do. She knew much of Surim's background. He had not had love as a child. His parents didn't sound as if they had been in love. He had nothing to show him the way. Could she? Dared she take a chance? It was her life on the line. And potential happiness. Or potential heartbreak.

Surim drove through the dark streets. He felt curiously numb. He'd asked Melissa to marry him after seeing Yasine tonight. The young woman had expressed her concern for Nadia, but she didn't even know her. She was showing him how compassionate she would be should she be chosen as his wife.

His aides kept him informed about the gossip around certain circles. He'd known Delleah wanted to marry him. Had Mara not died and left him guardian of her children, maybe he and Delleah would have made a match. She was beautiful.

As was Yasine.

As was Melissa.

He was stunned she'd refused him. He thought he caught a glimpse of emotion sometimes when they were together. He knew he wanted to spend time with her every day. He loved talking with Melissa on any topic. She was bright, articulate, had definite opinions. And she could make him laugh. Sometimes she did it deliberately, he knew. But other times he laughed for the pure joy of being with her. And when they kissed…

The road to his house came up, but he passed by heading for the sea.

She liked living here. The one certainty he had about Melissa was she wasn't a person to play games. If she liked something, she showed it. If not, she was clear on that as well.

When he reached the road that ran along the Gulf, he turned toward the restaurant he'd taken her to for lunch only two days ago. It seemed a lifetime ago. Nadia's sudden illness had changed everything. Put things into perspective, he'd thought. Melissa would make a perfect mother. She loved those children. Her refusal had to mean she didn't care enough about him to stay.

Which hurt.

Surim was surprised to realize that was the emotion that filled him. He wanted her and she didn't want him.

The story of his life, it seemed. He should be used to it by now. But he had thought she was different.

Reaching the restaurant's car park, he pulled in and cut the engine. The silence was broken only by the soft soughing of the wavelets as they splashed against the shore. The night was dark, stars littered the sky. But Surim saw nothing, gazing out into the darkness, feeling the night reflect how he felt. Dark and silent.

Dawn was breaking when he started the engine again. He'd

thought long and hard about the situation, but could find no resolution. If Melissa had her way, she'd be gone soon and he and the children would be left alone.

Unless he took drastic steps.

He reached home in record time. After a quick shower and change of clothes, he was ready for the day. Heading for his office, he placed a call to Max.

"Hello?" a rough voice answered the phone.

"Max? Surim here."

"Do you know what time it is? It's in the middle of the night. What's wrong?"

"Sorry, forgot the time change. I need to talk with you."

"Now? Is it an emergency? Did something happen to the restaurant? Don't tell me the thing burned up. I thought we were on schedule for the opening."

"It's not about the restaurant."

"Then what the hell do you need to talk to me about at two o'clock in the morning?"

"Melissa."

"What? Is something wrong with her? She's all right, isn't she?"

"She's fine. I need some advice, actually."

"About?"

Surim wasn't sure he wanted to confess the next part, but he needed Max's input.

"I asked her to marry me and she said no."

There was silence on the line for a long moment. Then, "You asked her to marry you? Why?"

"She's blended in perfectly here. She's terrific with the children. Thanks to her demands, I've come to know those kids and love them. I can't imagine not having them as part of my life now. I know we wouldn't have come to this without her."

Surim took a breath, waiting to hear what Max would have

to say. If he laughed or made some sarcastic comment, Surim would take the next plane to London to settle with his friend.

But Max didn't say anything for a few seconds.

"Is that it?" Max asked.

"She'd be perfect."

"Surim, she's a woman. What's in it for her?"

"She'd be my wife; isn't that enough?"

"Nice, if that's what she wants. From the little I've seen of Melissa, and I don't know her that well, material things don't seem to figure high in her scheme of life. She values relationships. How do you feel about that?"

"I want her."

"Yeah, she's a looker all right. But more than that?"

"What more?"

"I know men aren't big on expressing emotions; my sisters tell me that all the time. But isn't there something missing from your big declaration? Something like love?"

"That's a western myth. In Qu'Arim we arrange marriages. And they are highly successful. We have a very low rate of divorce."

"Quote her that, why don't you?"

"I have."

Max laughed. "God, Surim, you're a piece of work. I'd have liked to have been there to hear her response."

"I have to marry to assure the succession. Why not to someone I want?"

"And Melissa is that someone?"

"Yes."

"Tell her."

"I did, and she refused me. Max, you're English, you'd have a better handle on what I should do to convince her to marry me. I would have no difficulties if she was from here."

"Tell me all the reasons you think this marriage would work," Max said.

Surim listed the aspects of being with Melissa that he liked. He talked about the evenings they'd spent together, the delight he felt around her.

"So now tell me what it would be like to have her gone from your life," Max said some time later.

After a moment, Surim shook his head. "I cannot."

"Why not?"

"Because I can't imagine her not being a part of my life."

When the doctor arrived, Melissa had been up all night. Nadia had wakened a short time earlier and eaten all the breakfast the nurse had brought. Her temperature was back to normal and her eyes looked bright again. She smiled at Melissa and was restless, wanting to get down.

The doctor examined her and smiled.

"She is better," he said.

Melissa knew that. Nadia had awakened with her normal zest for activity and running around, and it was hard to keep her in the bed or hold her.

"So she can go home today?" Melissa asked.

"One more day, just to make sure. But I'm certain she is on the road to full recovery. Children this young get sick suddenly, but recover almost as quickly."

Melissa was so happy to see the little girl look like her normal self again. She could hardly wait for Surim to hear the good news. She asked the nurse to contact him.

"So, little one, you're going to be fine," Melissa said to Nadia when the doctor and his entourage left. "Soon we'll be back home." Melissa stopped suddenly. They'd return home, but she had plans to make. Who would take care of these lovely children? Would Annis be enough now? They'd had too many changes in a short time.

By mid-afternoon, Melissa realized Surim wasn't coming to the hospital. She'd had the nurse phone him again, and taken the receiver to speak to him directly. She wanted some of the books Nadia liked. And maybe a couple of toys to counter her restlessness now that she was feeling better.

He was not there, but the person answering rang her through to Annis who promised to send the requested items.

"How are the other children doing?" Melissa asked.

"They went with Surim today. They were all overjoyed with the good news," Annis said. "As was I."

For a little while Melissa thought Surim might be bringing the others to visit Nadia, but when one of the servants arrived with her books and toys Melissa gave up on that idea.

Where would Surim have taken the children?

By the time Nadia went to sleep that evening, Melissa was ready to drop. The nurse urged her to get some rest, reminding her that the next day Nadia was to be released and Melissa could scarcely care for her at home if she was too exhausted to even stay awake.

She reluctantly agreed. Before long the limousine had been summoned and Melissa sat in solitary splendor in the back, dozing on the ride to Surim's home.

When she arrived, the lights were on, but upon entering she found the house was silent.

She went upstairs, wanting to check on Alaya and Hamid.

Miracle of miracles, they were both asleep, and it wasn't even nine o'clock.

Going to her room, Melissa quickly showered and crawled into bed. She hadn't seen Surim today and already missed him with an aching that wouldn't go away. Was this how she would spend the next week and months and years without him?

The next morning when Melissa rose, the sun was shining as brightly as almost every other morning she'd been in Qu'Arim. She dressed, anxious to see Alaya and Hamid, and then go to the hospital to get Nadia. She went up to the nursery, surprised to see Surim already at the table with the children.

"You got the message about Nadia, according to Annis," she said, entering the room, trying to quell the sheer delight seeing him brought.

"I did. We will all go to get her at nine. I have already spoken with her physician this morning," Surim said. "Before we go, however, I wish to speak to you in the study downstairs. After we eat."

"Sure." Melissa greeted the children and soon sat down to eat her breakfast, wondering what Surim would have to say. Was he arranging a flight home for her right away so not to hinder her departure? Or would he try again to talk her into staying? It proved awkward to be with him after refusing his proposal. Her heart fluttered with apprehension. Either way, she was on tenterhooks until their meeting.

He escorted her down the two flights of stairs, not saying a word. They walked into the study and he closed the door. Without another word, he pulled her into his arms and kissed her.

She clung with abandonment, returning each caress and touch, running her fingers through his thick hair, holding on tightly for the exquisite sensations that threatened to explode. She'd missed him so much last night. Yearned to see him.

"I'm so relieved Nadia is getting better," he said a moment later, resting his forehead against hers. "Thank you for your devotion, Melissa. I've hired a nurse to watch her for a few days, just to make sure she's all right."

"Annis and I could have managed."

"I know. But there is no need. We will bring her home, then, before you leave, I want to show you something. The oasis I told you about."

Her heart dropped. Was this his gesture of farewell?

Swallowing the lump in her throat, she smiled. "I should love to see the oasis. But shouldn't I stay with Nadia?"

"As I said, she'll be safe with the nurse and Annis. We will wait another day and then fly to the interior."

Melissa held onto her smile, hoping it reached her eyes and that the sadness she felt wasn't evident. She wanted to run to her room and shut the door and pretend everything was as it had been a week ago.

Surim established the nurse in charge of the sick room. The little girl made rapid recovery. He went to see her that evening, reading to her and staying until after she fell asleep. Watching her sleep, he was filled with love. How wise of Melissa to make sure he and the children got to know each other. He couldn't imagine his life without them now. Any more than he could imagine it without Melissa. But if he didn't change her mind, that was exactly what he faced.

Early Wednesday morning, Surim escorted Melissa to a private airport near the capital's huge commercial airport.

"We're taking a private plane?" she asked when he parked near the small terminal.

"I have a plane I keep here. It'll take us to Wadi Serene."

"Wadi Sarene?"

"The name of the oasis."

"It has an airport?" Melissa pictured the place in the middle of the desert, alone and isolated. How far off was her imagination if it had an airport?

"No, we'll land in a nearby town, and then drive to the oasis."

When they walked to the plane, Melissa realized Surim was the pilot. She was fascinated by this side of him and watched avidly as he did the preflight check, burning every moment into memory. The flight itself was different from the big jets she was used to. They could see the city, and watch as it gradually gave way to less-populated areas until they were flying over golden sands. Here and there were settlements, mostly surrounding oil derricks. Surim pointed out the sights and gave her a running history of his country as they flew west. Soon even those scattered settlements were left behind and only the timeless desert unfolded beneath them.

Some time later Surim pointed out the small group of buildings in the distance. Slowly they drew closer as he descended. The airport was a packed dirt runway with a bright orange air sock indicating the wind direction. He brought the plane down in a soft landing and taxied to the small building that served as the terminal.

"That was fabulous!" she exclaimed as she stepped from the small plane. "I was able to see so much of Qu'Arim."

"From a distance. Come, the Jeep there is mine."

"Kept ready in case you drop by?" she asked as she walked beside him to the car.

"No, I called ahead to arrange things. It should be packed with food and supplies for tonight and tomorrow."

It was almost sunset before they reached the oasis. A small stand of palm trees rose from the desert. When they drew closer, Melissa saw the huge tent near the trees, and even heard the bubbling of the spring.

A breeze blew, cooling the air, highlighting the silence of the expanse. In every direction she looked, Melissa only saw empty desert. She and Surim were alone.

"It's beautiful," she said softly, drinking in the serenity and peace.

"I like it." He pulled the Jeep near the tent and stopped.

The canvas structure was unlike any Melissa had seen before. It had to be at least twenty feet long, with flaps tied back as if unveiling a masterpiece. She got out and headed for the opening, pausing a moment in the archway, then stepping in. She felt like Alice.

The interior was unexpected. Thick Persian carpets covered the sand. Chairs and a table were to one side, already set for a meal. A bowl of fruit spilling over. A divan with plump pillows sat in the back. A low brass table before it. Hanging panels of rich tapestries divided the sleeping areas from the main part. Brass lamps glowed, illuminating the space, though the sunlight still seeped in through the opening.

Turning, she smiled in enchantment. "This is the most fantastic thing I've ever seen," she whispered.

Surim came to stand beside her, looking around his tent as if through her eyes.

"The tent reminds me of our roots. The interior of how far we've come."

"Thank you for bringing me. I shall never forget it."

He gazed into her eyes. "I'm hoping you'll come again. I've never brought anyone else here, Melissa. It's my special place. I never thought I'd share it. But I wanted you to see it, hopefully to like it. It's somewhere we can escape to when life gets too complicated.

"Marry me, Melissa. Spend your days and nights with me. Grow old with me."

"Surim." How could she continue to refuse? Yet how could she settle? Wasn't that a mistake?

"After careful consideration and consultation, I have to admit I had not fully thought through my proposal at the hospital. Now I have and can say with all assurance that I love you."

"What? Impossible!" She stared at him, astonished. That was the last thing she'd expected him to say.

His eyes danced in amusement at her response. "Why so?"

"You don't believe in love."

"*Didn't.* I've had it pointed out to me clearly that the tangle of emotions I feel for you are all combined in one called love."

"Who pointed it out?"

"Max."

"You talked to Max Valentine about me?"

Surim kissed her gently, then passionately. It was some time before Melissa could speak again. But once she could, she narrowed her eyes as she looked up at him.

"So you think you love me?"

"I do," he said.

"Since when?"

"I believe since the night you started making demands in exchange for agreeing to stay."

"That first week?"

"You have fascinated me from the beginning. Then enticed me. Then beguiled me."

"I don't know what to say."

"Try, Yes, Surim, I will marry you."

"It's about the children, isn't it?"

"No. This is about you and me. The children will grow up and move out. I want you with me as long as I live. I love you, Melissa. Say you love me."

She was silent, trying to believe, feeling the warmth of his words fill her, the honesty of his tone reaching her. Her heart felt as if it would burst with happiness.

"Oh, Surim, if you're sure you love me, I'll marry you in a heartbeat. I love you beyond anything!"

The gleam in his eyes shone as he caught her in his embrace and kissed her again.

"Affection grows in marriage," he said, "but I didn't expect to feel such strong passion before."

"Love explodes," she said, hugging him hard. "Are you sure? I've loved you for weeks, but hid it because you were going to marry some suitable woman approved by the Qu'Arim ministers."

"You are now in Qu'Arim and I'm marrying you and no one else. And we'll get the ministers to celebrate the marriage. What more could we want?"

"I'm not so suitable."

"If I say you are most suitable, who is going to argue with me?" he countered.

Melissa laughed joyfully. She didn't know of anyone who would argue with the sheikh of Qu'Arim. Certainly not her—at least on this subject.

He took a deep breath and held her close. "I want you, Melissa. I want you in my bed every night, you and me and nothing in between. I want to make love to you until we are both too old to remember what it means. I want you at breakfast, chiding me about neglecting the children. I want you at dinner, making sure the children practice good manners. And in the evening when it's just you and me reviewing our day, I want to see you in pearls, and laughing with me, and looking at me with the love in your eyes that you give so freely to the children."

Her heart began to pound.

"I want you with all the passion in my soul. I never thought I'd care for anyone the way I do you. I've come to love those children, but it doesn't hold a candle to what I feel for you. When Max asked me to envision my life without you, I could not do it. You have become a part of me. I can promise you I'll love you and be faithful forever. I'll do all in my power to keep you happy throughout all our life together."

"Oh, Surim," she whispered. The man who had lacked so much in his life was promising to make hers wondrous beyond belief. "I thought you wanted me for the children."

"I want to have children with you—a little girl with her mother's green eyes. Or a little boy to grow in the ways of our culture to assume a leadership role some day. Or become a doctor if he'd prefer."

"What?"

He smiled. "I'll explain another time. I do want children, Melissa, but only with you. And once they are grown, it'll be you and me for the rest of our lives. I couldn't imagine spending those years without you. I love you; how can I prove it?"

"You have no need to prove anything. I believe you. And I love you too." She had tears in her eyes at his impassioned declaration. Her heart was overflowing. He'd brought her, and only her, to his special place, this magical oasis. He'd proposed to her as she'd never dreamed of being asked. Her heart was so full she could hardly stand it.

"So, what do you think about our life together?" he asked, gently brushing an escaping tear from her cheek.

"I want all that as well," she replied simply, glowing with love for him and the future he painted. 'As long as you love me forever.'

"Forever and a day," he said, kissing her to show her just how much.

* * * * *

Louise Valentine is still smarting from the humiliation of being fired from Bella Lucia by her workaholic cousin Max, and the discovery that she was adopted as a child. Then, Max turns up on the doorstep of her successful PR and Marketing company, insisting that she do some promotions work for the family's restaurant chain. At first Louise coldly rebuffs him—but then she finds that years of secret longing for Max cannot be forgotten so easily...

Here's an exclusive extract...

"So WHY are you so anxious to have me come and work for you?"

Because he was crazy, he thought.

Who did he think he was kidding? Working with Louise was going to try his self-control to its limits.

He took a slow breath.

"I want you to work *with* me, Lou, not *for* me. I respect your skill, your judgment, but we both know that I could buy that out in the marketplace. What makes you special, unique, is that you've spent a lifetime breathing in the very essence of Bella Lucia. You're a Valentine to your fingertips, Louise. The fact that you're adopted doesn't alter any of that."

"It alters how I feel."

"I understand that and, for what it's worth, I think Ivy and John were wrong not to tell you the truth, but it doesn't change who or what you are. Jack wants you on board, Louise, and he's right."

"He's been chasing you? Wants to know why you haven't signed me up yet? Well, that would explain your sudden enthusiasm."

"He wanted to know the situation before he took off last week."

"Took off? Where's he gone?"

"He was planning to meet up with Maddie in Florence at the weekend. To propose to her."

"You're kidding!" And when he shook his head, "Oh, but that's so romantic!" Then, apparently recalling the way he'd flirted with Maddie at the Christmas party, she said, "Are you okay with that?"

He found her concern unexpectedly touching. "More than okay," he assured her. "I was only winding Jack up at Christmas. It's what brothers do."

"You must have really put the wind up him if he was driven to marriage," she said.

"Bearing in mind our father's poor example, I think you can be sure that he wouldn't have married her unless he loved her, Lou."

Or was he speaking for himself?

"No. Of course not. I'm sorry."

Sorry? Louise apologizing to him? That had to be a first. Things were looking up.

She laughed.

"What?"

She shook her head. "Weddings to the left of us, weddings to the right of us and not one of them held at a family restaurant." She tutted. "You know what you need, Max? Some heavyweight marketing muscle."

"I'm only interested in the best, Louise, so why don't we stop pussyfooting around, wasting time when we could be planning for the future?" The thought of an entire evening with her teasing him, drawing out concessions one by one, exacting repayment for every time he'd let her down, every humiliation, was enough to bring him out in a cold sweat. "Why don't you tell me what it's going to cost me? Your bottom line."

"You don't want to haggle?"

Definitely teasing.

"You want to see me suffer, is that it? If I call it total surrender, will that satisfy your injured pride?"

Her smile was as enigmatic as anything the Mona Lisa could offer. "Total surrender might be acceptable," she told him.

"You've got it. So, what's your price?"

"Nothing."

He stared at her, shocked out of teasing. That was it? A cold refusal?

"Nothing?" Then, when she didn't deny it, "You mean that this has all been some kind of elaborate wind-up? That you're not even going to consider my proposal?"

"As a proposal it lacked certain elements."

"Money? You know what you're worth, Louise. We're not going to quibble over a consultancy fee."

She shook her head. "No fee."

Outside the taxi the world moved on, busy, noisy. Commuters crossing en masse at the lights, the heavy diesel engine of a bus in the next lane, a distant siren. Inside it was still, silent, as if the world were holding its breath.

"No fee?" he repeated.

"I'll do what you want, Max. I'll give you—give the family—my time. It won't cost you a penny."

He didn't fall for it. Nothing came without some cost.

"You can't work without being paid, Louise."

"It's not going to be forever. I'll give you my time until… until the fourteenth. Valentine's Day. The diamond anniversary of the founding of Bella Lucia."

"Three weeks. Is that all?"

"It's all I can spare. My reward is my freedom, Max. I owe the family and I'll do this for them. Then the slate will be wiped clean."

"No…"

He didn't like the sound of that. He didn't want her for just a few weeks. Didn't want to be treated like a client, even if he was getting her time for nothing. Having fought the idea for so long, he discovered that he wanted more, a lot more from her than that.

"You're wrong. You can't just walk away, replace one family with another. You can't wipe away a lifetime of memories, of care—"

"It's the best deal you're ever likely to get," she said, cutting him short before he could add "of love…"

"Even so. I can't accept it."

"You don't have a choice," she said. "You asked for my bottom line; that's it."

"There's always a choice," he said, determined that she shouldn't back him into a corner, use Bella Lucia as a salve to her conscience, so that she could walk away without a backward glance. Something that he knew she'd come to regret.

Forget Bella Lucia.

This was more important and, if he did nothing else, he had to stop her from throwing away something so precious.

"That's my offer, Max. Take it or leave it."

"There must be something that you want, that I can offer you," he said, assailed by a gut-deep certainty that he must get her to accept something from them—from him. Make it more than a one way transaction. For her sake as much as his. "Not money," he said, quickly, "if that's the way you want it, but a token."

"A token? Anything?"

Her eyes were leaden in the subdued light of the cab, making it impossible to read what she was thinking. That had changed. There had been a time when every thought had been written across her face, as easy to read as a book.

He was going into this blind.

"Anything," he said.

"You insist?"

He nodded once.

"Then my fee for working with you on the expansion of the Bella Lucia restaurant group, Max, is…a kiss."

* * * * *

Don't miss this sizzling finale to The Brides of Bella Lucia
Liz Fielding's
THE VALENTINE BRIDE (#3934)
out in February 2007
*Find out whether Max and Louise can put their turbulent
past behind them and find a future together.*